*Leigh Michaels has written
over 70 books for Harlequin Romance®
and her books are loved by women
the world over.*

Praise for Leigh Michaels

"Leigh Michaels is sure to charm readers of
Harlequin Romance."
—*www.thebestreviews.com*

"Leigh Michaels's fresh and fiery characters
have universal appeal."
—*www.romantictimes.com*

"When you sit down with [a Leigh Michaels book],
you're definitely in for a very pleasant
and entertaining adventure!"
—*www.thebestreviews.com*

Leigh loves to hear from readers. You may contact her
at: P.O. Box 935, Ottumwa, Iowa 52501, U.S.A.
or visit her Web site: leigh@leighmichaels.com

Leigh Michaels has always been a writer, composing dreadful poetry when she was just four years old and dictating it to her long-suffering older sister. She started writing romance in her teens and burned six full manuscripts before submitting her work to a publisher. Now, with more than 75 novels to her credit, she also teaches romance writing seminars at universities, writers' conferences and on the Internet.

Books by Leigh Michaels

THE HUSBAND
SWEEPSTAKE

Leigh Michaels

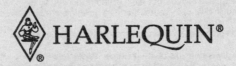

HARLEQUIN®

TORONTO • NEW YORK • LONDON
AMSTERDAM • PARIS • SYDNEY • HAMBURG
STOCKHOLM • ATHENS • TOKYO • MILAN • MADRID
PRAGUE • WARSAW • BUDAPEST • AUCKLAND

ISBN 0-373-03815-1

THE HUSBAND SWEEPSTAKE

First North American Publication 2004.

www.eHarlequin.com

Printed in U.S.A.

CHAPTER ONE

THE trip had been more fast-paced than usual. Erika had crammed at least three weeks' worth of work into a mere ten days, and even a good night's sleep in her own bed hadn't been enough for her to fully recuperate from exhaustion and jet lag. It was barely ten in the morning—at least that was what the tiny gold watch on her wrist said, though her body clock wasn't anywhere near so certain of the hour. Nevertheless, she was patting back a yawn as the elevator reached the lobby.

That will never do, she thought. With her schedule already crammed with meetings and her in-basket no doubt overflowing, she didn't have time to be tired. Not today.

She felt as if she'd been gone for a month. Winter had abruptly let go its hold on New York City while she'd been gone. The last traces of dirty snow had melted away, and though it had been almost dusk, she thought she'd glimpsed the first hints of green in Central Park on her way home from the airport yesterday. Even the building's lobby looked a little different than when she'd left. This morning sunshine poured in through the beveled glass around the main doors, sprinkling jewel-colored patches across the freshly cleaned carpet.

But some things never changed, Erika thought fondly as she walked across the lobby to the small office tucked into a corner next to the elevators.

Inside, with his back to the door as he leaned over a table studying a clipboard full of papers, was—in Erika's view—probably the single best thing about living in this newly renovated apartment complex. According to the nameplate on the door, Stephen was the manager of the complex, in charge of rentals, deposits, repairs and tenant complaints. But in fact the job he'd carved out for himself in the eight months since the complex opened was more like that of the concierge of a first-class hotel. Need tickets to the symphony? Talk to Stephen—he had contacts everywhere. Need the dog walked? Talk to Stephen—he knew someone who'd be great at the job. Need someone to let the delivery people in with the new couch? Talk to Stephen; he'd not only sign the paperwork but make sure they moved all the furniture to just the right angle…

Yes, *definitely* the best thing about living here, Erika told herself. "Stephen, darling—"

The man at the table stood up straighter and started to turn to face her.

The instant he moved, Erika knew that she'd made a big mistake. Where Stephen was jittery in his movements, this man was slow and smooth, like a panther on the prowl. He was a little taller than Stephen, too—an inch or two, perhaps—and his hair was just a shade darker.

She should have recognized the difference the moment she walked in—though, she reminded herself, there was no reason to scourge herself for making a simple mistake. She was used to finding Stephen in this office, and she wasn't used to seeing him from behind. So it was no wonder she hadn't immediately identified this man as a stranger.

He'd turned all the way around now, and she got her first good look at his face. Now she could see that he wasn't at all like Stephen, really—not only was his hair darker, almost black in fact, but it was thicker, curlier, and more unruly than Stephen's. His eyes weren't brown like Stephen's but as rich a blue as Long Island Sound on a hot summer's day, and they looked just as deep and inviting.

He wasn't exactly handsome, but there was something about him which invited a second look. His face was full of healthy color, but he didn't have the deep sun-bronzed shade that Stephen somehow managed to sport even in the depths of winter.

And though he was wearing the same type of dark suit and ascot tie that Stephen favored, it didn't fit him the same way. The formal garb didn't look out of place on him, and yet it seemed somehow uncomfortable, as if he wasn't used to dressing up.

"I'm not Stephen," he said.

As if she wouldn't be able to figure that out on her own. Erika felt like rolling her eyes.

He added, not quite under his breath, "...darling."

Erika opened her mouth to blister him for impudence, and then decided that it would be more effective in the long run just to ignore him. "I can see that," she said sweetly. "So where's Stephen?"

"I can page him if you like, Ms. Forrester."

She didn't ask how he knew her name. She didn't need to.

He went on easily, "I believe he's helping Mr. Richards locate his missing snake up on the third floor."

Erika shivered. "Then I certainly don't want to disturb him."

His eyes gleamed with laughter. Erika was sure of it, even though the expression was gone almost as quickly as it had appeared. She was intrigued despite herself. "And who are you?" she asked.

"I'm Stephen's new assistant."

"I gathered that from the uniform." She waved a finger in the direction of his ascot. "He could certainly use a helper. Or perhaps I should say that the residents could use two Stephens."

He looked down at the dark suit as if not quite believing what he was wearing. "He does seem to keep himself busy."

"And your name?" He didn't answer immediately, so Erika prodded, "In case Stephen's not here, it would be handy to know who I'm talking to."

"If it's not Stephen," he pointed out gently, "it'll be me. But you can call me Amos—" He bit off the sentence, leaving the name hanging.

Erika was absolutely certain the word he'd swallowed hadn't been a last name at all. He'd actually almost had the cheek to say she could call him *Amos darling.* But at least he'd maintained enough sense to zip the lip before he'd finished, while she could still pretend not to have heard. It was much less embarrassing for both of them that way.

"I'll tell him you stopped by. I'm sure he'll be heartbroken to have missed you," Amos said, and started to turn back to the clipboard he'd been looking at when she came in.

Just who does this guy think he is? she thought. "Well, let me fill you in on the routine around here. It's cleaning day, so—"

"Are you referring to the housecleaning service or the dry cleaners?" he interrupted politely. "I've already been instructed that since it's Tuesday, your housekeeping team will be arriving before long. And Stephen has made a note to arrange an extra laundry pickup today as well, since you just got home from your trip. So he already has all the usual things covered."

Erika eyed him for a long moment. The urge to squash him was rapidly becoming unbearable. She would have to either put him in his place, or walk out—and soon. "You know," she mused, "if you want to be successful around here, it might pay to take a few lessons from Stephen on customer service.''

His eyebrows lifted. ''But, Ms. Forrester, I was simply trying not to waste your time. Why should you have to repeat instructions that Stephen has already taken care of?'' He looked innocent, and he sounded solicitous.

Erika didn't believe an iota of it.

''I presumed you would rather have Stephen look after your needs, since he's already accustomed to your routine. But if there is anything you'd prefer me to do for you,'' he went on gently, ''you need only ask.''

She hitched her black leather tote bag higher onto her shoulder. ''I'll do my best to think of something,'' she murmured. ''Because I'd hate for you to feel at loose ends around here while Stephen's doing all the work.''

The brisk walk from her apartment complex to Ladylove's building in Midtown Manhattan refreshed Erika, and by the time she arrived at her office, she'd almost forgotten about *Amos darling*. He was hardly worth thinking about, anyway, she told herself. With that kind of attitude, he wouldn't last long around an upscale apartment complex, no matter how pleasant he was to look at.

The tapestry-lined elevator whooshed Erika to the top floor. In her corner office, her personal assistant was just setting a steaming cappuccino beside the pile of already-opened mail on the blotter.

Erika checked on the threshold. ''How do you do it, Kelly? Always have a fresh cup waiting for me when I come in?''

The little redhead grinned, her gamin face alight with mischief. ''The company spy network, of course. Didn't you realize how efficient it is?'' She took Erika's trench coat and hung it in the small closet. ''You have an appointment with your personal fitter this morning, by the way. She's bringing over some dresses so you can choose one to wear to the banquet Saturday night.''

''See if you can catch her before she leaves the store. I need a white silk blouse, too, because I spilled a glass of red wine on mine when I was in Rome.'' Erika frowned. ''Wait a minute. What banquet? There's nothing like that on my calendar.''

''Not officially, but then you've been out of the office for more than a week. The invitation came while you were gone. However, since last Friday's *Sentinel* announced that you'll be attending, I thought it best to be prepared—so I sent a check for two tickets, and I called the fitter about a dress.''

''Sometimes,'' Erika muttered, ''I'd like to do the opposite, just to spite the tabloids.''

Kelly shook her head. ''Issuing a challenge like that would only make them more interested. Then they'd run stories about you every day instead of only two or three times a week. Besides, the banquet is for a good cause.''

''They're all good causes, Kelly.'' Erika sat down behind the graceful Georgian table which she used as a desk. ''Has the *Sentinel* announced yet where I'm going on my summer vacation? I can't make up my mind, but I'm sure they've already figured out what I'll decide.'' She sipped the cappuccino and flipped through the mail.

Kelly clicked her tongue. ''It's a wee bit early in the day to be sounding cynical, now.''

''And it's a wee bit too far from Dublin for you to be using a brogue.''

''Not if it makes you laugh. One plain white silk blouse, coming up. And Erika—I know how you feel about the *Sentinel,* but you should read today's edition anyway.''

Kelly pulled the office door closed behind her, and Erika

sank back in her chair and reached for the neatly folded newspaper at the bottom of the stack of mail. At least she could find out what the good cause was that she would be supporting by going to a banquet on Saturday.... No, Kelly had said that story had run last week. In any case, the red-head's voice had sounded almost too casual—as if she was issuing some kind of a warning. So what horrible thing had New York City's most-highly-circulated gossip sheet said about her this time?

Or had they just gotten hold of a photo that was more terrible than usual? Erika had thought, herself, that the one which had first appeared a couple of weeks ago—the one which seemed to have become the editor's favorite—would be impossible to top. She'd been chewing a bite of arugula when the paparazzi's flash went off in her face, and she thought the result had made her look like a serial murderer with a toothache.

But for a change her own face didn't jump out at her as she scanned the pages. She frowned and started over from the beginning.

She found the story, finally, on page six. It was no wonder she hadn't seen it before, because this time it wasn't about her—not directly, at least. The story was an engagement announcement and the photograph which accompanied it was of a dimpled, childlike woman and a man Erika barely recognized. And the editors had waited till the very last paragraph to point out that the prospective groom had been engaged before—to Erika.

She sipped her cappuccino and read the story again, slowly and thoughtfully.

Denby Miles's previous engagement was to Erika Forrester, who was then the trademark face (and is now also the CEO) of Ladylove Cosmetics. The match was broken off shortly after Erika's father, Stanford Forrester III, completed the purchase of Mr. Miles's portfolio of perfume formulae to add to Ladylove's armory. There was and continues to be some speculation about the timing of the breakup.

"What she did to him stank worse than Denby's perfumes," one society matron—who wished to remain anonymous—told the Sentinel. *"Leading him on just to get those chemical formulas, and then dropping him flat. I'm just glad the poor boy is finally over his broken heart."*

Erika folded the paper and flung it as hard as she could. It slammed against the office door and flopped onto the carpet.

The door opened a crack, and Kelly peeked warily through the opening. "Does that mean I shouldn't clip this one for your scrapbook?"

Erika said grimly, "Remind me to send the *Sentinel's* editors a gift next Christmas. A new sledgehammer—because at this rate they'll have worn out the one they're using now."

"Yeah, I thought that line about Denby's perfumes stinking was a little low," Kelly agreed. She picked up the paper and smoothed the ruffled pages. "There are a couple of his scents which really aren't bad at all."

Erika tried to bite back a grin. "Well, no wonder their source wanted to remain nameless, saying things like that. It was probably Denby's mother. Honestly, Kelly, what did I ever do to annoy the tabloids so much?"

"You seriously don't know?" Kelly perched on the arm of a chair. "Think about it, Erika. A supposedly brainless blond makeup model takes over her father's business and—instead of falling flat on her gorgeous face—makes more of a success of it than he ever did. *That's* what you did to annoy them. You didn't stay in the slot they'd picked for you."

"Well, wouldn't you think they'd give it up by now? It's two years since I broke that engagement, and since my father died."

"And every time a new Ladylove ad comes out, your picture reminds them of how wrong they were. Enjoy it, Erika. It's a measurement of your success."

"Sort of like being named the Chamber of Commerce's Man of the Year? I'll try to keep that in mind." Erika picked up her pen. "By the way, Kelly, about that banquet Saturday night—have either you or the *Sentinel* decided who I'm going with?"

"They haven't said." Kelly maintained a deadpan expression. "And I thought it should be your choice."

"That's reassuring. Which good cause am I supporting?"

"Adult literacy, I believe."

"Literacy? I wish I understood how my eating rubbery chicken and listening to a speaker drone on all evening is supposed to help the cause of reading. Can you give me one good reason why I shouldn't just stay home and take a book to bed instead?"

By the time Erika paid off her cab in front of the apartment complex, Stephen was on the sidewalk to greet her. "Just the person I wanted to see," she said, handing him the blue-and-silver dress bag she was carrying.

"Welcome home, Ms. Forrester," he said as he ushered her into the lobby. "I was sorry to miss you when you arrived last night. There's fresh espresso in my office, if you'd like a cup."

"You're a love, Stephen." She sank into the guest's chair in his office—an extra-comfortable wing-back covered in a heathery tweed—and put her feet up on the small matching footstool, watching as he hung her dress bag next to an identical one on a hat stand beside the door. "This is wonderful. What happened to your assistant? Did you send him home for the night, or has he already quit?"

"Why would he quit?" Stephen looked puzzled.

Erika shrugged. "It seemed to me this morning that he was already a bit tired of the residents' oddities, so I'd be amazed if he stuck with it for long."

Stephen's gaze shifted a bit. "Oh, I think Amos will be around for a while," he said vaguely. "He just has a little different philosophy of the job than I do, that's all."

Understatement of the year, Erika thought.

"What can I do for you, Ms. Forrester?"

"I need advice," Erika said crisply. "Break out your little black address book and tell me which of your friends would like to go to a banquet with me on Saturday. Hear an inspiring speaker—"

Stephen shook his head. "I'm running out of friends who will fall for that one."

"There are benefits," Erika began.

From behind her, a pleasant voice asked, "A woman like you needs an escort service?"

Erika almost dropped the cup Stephen had just handed her. She twisted around to see Amos, who was lounging against the door with his arms folded across his chest.

Stephen sighed. "Amos, you can't just talk to the residents like—"

"I'm off duty." Amos strolled in and perched on the corner of the desk.

He certainly looked it, Erika thought. The dark suit and ascot were gone, replaced with faded jeans and a lightweight sweater with the sleeves pushed up to the elbows. His shoulders looked even broader, and the blue of his sweater made his eyes seem brighter.

"I've tried to explain," Stephen said wearily, "that on this job you're never off duty."

"Speak for yourself, Stephen. No wonder you're always tired. I want to hear why Ms. Forrester needs help finding a date. To say nothing of being curious about what she means by benefits."

It was obviously too late to pretend she'd been joking. Anyway, Erika asked herself, why should it bother her if *Amos darling* thought she couldn't attract a man without help? She looked him in the eye. "I don't know why you've got this chip on your shoulder, but if it's just me you have a problem with, I promise not to bother you anymore. In fact, I'll simply ignore you altogether. If you can convince enough of the residents to share my feelings, you'll have a pretty easy job of it—for however long it lasts. Now if you'll go away, *Amos darling,* and let me talk to Stephen in private—"

He didn't move. "Next time you want to talk to Stephen in private, shut the door. Half the building could have heard you, so why object because I happened to walk by?"

Stephen cleared his throat. "All right, let's get back to the point. What kind of a banquet is it and who will be there? If there are connections to be made, then maybe—"

"It's for adult literacy. So your friend can hang out with authors and publishers and readers and agents and—"

Stephen was smiling.

"You've thought of someone? Stephen, you're an angel."

Amos slid off the desk. "Now that you have the problem solved, I'll be—"

"It sounds right down Amos's alley," Stephen said.

Erika stared at him. "This is no time for a joke."

"I was serious. Amos is writing a book. That's why he's here."

Erika tipped her head to one side and inspected Amos. She thought she saw irritation flicker in his eyes.

Well, that makes two of us who are annoyed at being fixed up with each other. "Why he's here?" she repeated.

"I don't know what you mean."

It was Amos who answered. "There are certain advantages to the position. Living quarters supplied, no commuting to work, flexible hours. As long as I take care of the residents' needs, I can do what I like with the rest of my time. Namely, write."

"And if you can persuade the residents not to ask you for anything, you'll do even better. No, Stephen, I couldn't live with myself if I dragged a genius away from the Great American Novel to attend a boring dinner." Erika pushed herself up from the chair. "And I'm sure the genius agrees."

"Now that would depend on the benefits you were talking about," Amos murmured. "Exactly what do they include?"

In your dreams, Amos darling. Erika looked at the twin dress bags hanging on the hat rack. "Which one of these is mine, Stephen? I lost track when you hung them up."

"Let me guess," Amos said. "You brought home a white silk blouse, I presume?"

Erika was puzzled. "Yes, as a matter of fact, though that's not all I bought. How do you know—?"

"Because Stephen insisted that since the dry cleaner's deliveryman refused responsibility for your white silk blouse, you must have a new one immediately. So he sent me trekking all the way down to midtown to pick it up this afternoon."

"So I have two brand-new white silk blouses? That's hilarious."

"Very amusing," Amos said politely. "I suppose you'd like me to take the extra back tomorrow."

"It would seem to be the logical move. Actually, I'd prefer it if you'd trade it for a different shade, something like teal or periwinkle..."

"How about wine-red? That would be dead easy—I could just finish the job you did on the original."

"On second thought, just take the blouse back. Don't bother to get another. It would be very foolish of me to assume that you know your colors, so I might end up with something in flame-orange or fluorescent green." She picked up a bag in each hand, weighed them and hung the lighter one back on the hat stand. "It was very thoughtful of you to anticipate my needs, Stephen." She started toward the elevator, bag in hand.

A low voice stopped her in midstride just a few paces from the office door. "You're quite wrong, Stephen," she heard Amos say. "That woman doesn't need a manager looking after her. What she needs is a keeper."

The members' lounge at the Civic Club was never noisy or crowded, but on Wednesday as the lunch hour neared, the room was as full as Erika had ever seen it. She toyed with a glass of sherry and tried to force down the butterflies in her stomach while she waited for her guest to arrive.

You don't have any idea what you're doing, whispered a voice in the back of her mind.

The voice sounded a little like her father. Erika took a deep breath and another sip and tried not to listen.

You have no experience with buyouts and takeovers. You've been lucky so far, that's all—and it isn't going to last forever. Don't push it.

She reached for a business magazine which lay on a small table beside her. She'd grab for anything which might serve to deflect that belittling voice in her head.

Kelly had been right, she thought—at least, up to a point. The *Sentinel*'s editors weren't the only ones who'd been surprised when Erika had stepped into her father's shoes at Ladylove Cosmetics after his death. In fact, Erika herself had been pretty much amazed when she'd actually stood up and said she wanted the job.

Ladylove's board of directors had been dumbstruck, but they hadn't had much choice in the matter. Stanford Forrester III had made sure to maintain a controlling interest in his company, and as long as Erika was voting her father's stock, she was every bit as much in control as he had been.

Not that she was as certain of what she was doing. But then Stanford Forrester hadn't always been able to predict the future, either. He hadn't intended to give up control, even when he died. And if he'd had any idea how close that day was, Erika was convinced, he'd have revised his will—because the one thing Stanford Forrester would never have wanted was for Erika to run his precious company.

Don't worry your pretty head about business, dear. Your job is to smile for the camera...

Well, she'd proved him wrong. In the eight quarters since she'd become the CEO, Ladylove had shown steady growth in market share and profits. Now that her position was solidified, Erika was ready to spread her wings. It was time for Ladylove to grow in scope as well as sales and production, and buying Felix La Croix's business and rolling it into Ladylove's was a natural move.

All she had to do was convince Felix La Croix, make the deal, and pull the two companies into one solid unit.

Her sherry glass was empty. She looked around. There

was still no sign of Felix, and all the waiters appeared to be busy as well. She leaned back in her chair and closed her eyes to do some creative visualization. *Picture yourself as a success and you'll be one.*

She sensed someone standing very still directly in front of her chair, and she sat up quickly, embarrassed. Would her guest think she'd been taking a nap? "Felix, I'm so glad—"

But the man standing over her with feet braced and arms folded wasn't Felix La Croix. It was Denby Miles, her ex-fiancé.

She'd run into him from time to time, of course, in the two years since their engagement had been broken off. Manhattan society wasn't large enough to avoid someone absolutely, even if one wanted to—and she'd never gone out of her way in order to stay out of his path. But on the rare occasions when they'd come face-to-face, they'd been coolly polite, exchanging greetings and then quickly moving on. He had never sought her out before, as he so obviously had this time. And she'd never had the opportunity, or felt the need, to look him over closely—not since that day two years ago when she'd taken off his ring and handed it back to him.

He was wider now, but not solider. He looked as if he'd put on weight, but not muscle. A smile might have masked the added fullness in his face, Erika thought, but he wasn't smiling.

"Denby," she said. "What a nice surprise to see you here at lunchtime."

His eyes narrowed. "What's that supposed to mean?"

"Exactly what I said. If a simple greeting offends you, I—"

"It's what you're implying that offends me—that the

worker bee should be in the lab from nine-to-five, no excuses, no breaks. Well, things have changed a bit now."

"Yes, I saw the announcement that you're marrying your boss's daughter," Erika said calmly. "Congratulations are in order, I believe."

"Of course you saw the announcement. You just had to go and ruin it, didn't you?"

"Ruin? I'm afraid I don't understand what you mean."

"Why do you have to push yourself into everything? You couldn't even stay out of my engagement announcement!"

Erika's jaw dropped. "You actually think I *wanted* to be part of that story?"

"Jeanette's heartbroken. This is the most important thing in her life, and you had to trample all over it."

Erika stood up. "Well, she'd better get over it. I'm a part of your past, Denby. No matter how much we'd all like to, we can't just wipe that out. Of course, if your engagement is as important to you as it is to her, then she doesn't have a thing to worry about where I'm concerned."

"You just have to have all the attention, don't you? Being the face in the ads wasn't enough, you had to be the CEO, too. Then—"

"Look, Denby, it was not my idea to have the *Sentinel* dish it all out again for the enjoyment of the masses. If you'll excuse me—" She tried to slip past him, but he was blocking the way.

"Maybe I'm wrong," he conceded.

"Well, that's big of you."

"Maybe you don't want it brought up again, especially right now—when you're doing it again."

"Doing what? What are you talking about?"

"You know," he said thoughtfully, "I always believed it was your father's idea for you to lead me on. To draw me in with promises until he got what he wanted. But now I wonder who was really behind that scheme. Maybe it was your plan after all.''

His voice was growing louder, unnaturally so in the quiet lounge, and people were starting to stare.

Denby didn't pause. ''And because it worked so well with me, you're trying it again. Maybe I should warn Felix La Croix what he's getting into. Make sure he understands that you're only making up to him in order to get his business.''

''I am not making up to—''

''That's who you're meeting today, isn't it? Maybe I'll just stick around and be sure he knows the truth.''

''Denby, this is utterly ridiculous!''

''Or maybe I'll just tell the *Sentinel*,'' he mused. ''Yes, that's the ticket. It will have the same effect, and I understand they pay pretty well for tips.''

From the corner of her eye, Erika caught a swift movement, almost a blur. It was too fast to be any of the club's members, she thought. They were never in a hurry, not here.

Realization dawned, and she ducked—but it was too late. The photo flash popped directly in her eyes, almost blinding her for an instant.

The photographer held his camera above his head, shaking it in triumph as if it were a trophy. Then he dodged past a determined-looking waiter, out the archway from the lounge into the club lobby, and through the front door to the street.

Denby blinked and said stupidly, ''What was that?''

''The *Sentinel*,'' Erika said grimly. ''I'd suggest, if you want to claim a tipster's fee, that you'd better hurry—before the paparazzi beats you to it.''

She turned away, and the waiter who had tried to stop

the photographer stepped into her path. "Ms. Forrester, Mr. La Croix asked me to give you this." He held out a folded sheet of paper that she recognized as club stationery.

For a moment, she'd forgotten all about Felix La Croix and the reason for her lunch date, but the solidity of the heavy sheet of parchment in her hand brought it all back.

The note was brief and to the point. "I'm sure you understand why I didn't wish to be part of the show. I'll be in touch when I've had a chance to think things through." It was signed with his initials.

Felix La Croix had been there, witnessed Denby's little act and opted to walk out. She couldn't exactly blame him for fading away rather than letting himself be drawn into the scene. At least he'd left a note.

"Will you be coming into the dining room now, Ms. Forrester?" the waiter asked.

Her stomach turned at the very idea of food. "No—thank you, Harry." She retrieved her portfolio from her chair and her trench coat from the cloakroom, stuffing Felix's note into her pocket. There was plenty to be done back at the office...

Except that right now she didn't feel like facing Kelly and fending off questions about how the negotiations had gone and why she was back so early.

She'd go home and lie down, she decided. It was only a few blocks to the apartment complex, and Stephen was guaranteed to have something on hand to settle an unhappy stomach.

But Stephen wasn't in the office; Amos was. A sandwich lay on the desk blotter, and beside it was a yellow legal tablet filled with scrawled and scratched-out sentences.

Erika checked on the threshold. "Sorry. I didn't mean to interrupt." She started to back out.

He stood up. "Come in. What can I do for you?"

Her head was still spinning; that must be why she had the sense that he actually sounded friendly. "What hit you? You sound positively civil. Oh, I know. You've decided you wouldn't mind going to that banquet after all—rubbing elbows with publishers and famous authors."

"I told you, it depends on the benefits. You look as if you just lost your last friend."

Erika sighed. "Do you have something for heartburn?"

He waved a hand toward the sandwich. "Italian sausage, onion and Swiss cheese. If that doesn't do it, nothing will."

"I meant something to treat it, not cause it." She swayed a little.

Amos seized her arm and guided her toward the wing-backed chair.

"I'm fine, really," Erika protested. "I just lost my balance, that's all. I'm not going to faint."

"In any case, sitting down won't hurt you a bit. What's the matter?"

"Oh, nothing much," she said lightly. "A ghost from the past, paparazzi popping out from the potted plants at what's supposed to be the most private club in the city, and a business deal gone sour."

"Well, I'm glad it wasn't anything important." He pushed aside the sandwich.

She pointed to the tablet. "Is that your book?"

He frowned at the scratched-out sentences. "A small piece of it."

"How's it going?"

"Slowly. Too many interruptions."

"I could have told you that. This may look like an easy job, but it's not."

"Only because Stephen has spoiled all of you."

"And especially me," Erika said steadily. "You might

as well say it as think it. Though I don't see why you said I needed a keeper.''

"What you need is a combination ladies' maid, secretary and bodyguard. It would fall more along the lines of a wife, actually.''

"A *wife?*"

"Yes, I think that covers it." He sounded quite pleased with himself.

"And that's your definition of a wife? My goodness, you have a twisted view of the world... Though come to think of it..."

Something was nagging at her. *Ladies' maid, secretary and bodyguard...*

She had the secretary, and she was perfectly capable of picking up her own clothes. But the bodyguard...

"You know, I think you've hit on something," she said. "Not a wife, of course—that would really give the tabloids something to talk about. But a husband...now that's another thing entirely. Amos—darling—what do you think?"

CHAPTER TWO

AMOS could think of only one reason why she could possibly want to know what he thought of her harebrained scheme. The explanation was ridiculous, it was insane, it was nigh impossible. But it was the only one he could come up with which even began to cover all the facts.

He stared across the desk at Erika, still trying to convince himself that she hadn't really said what he thought he'd heard. She was perfectly calm, her violet eyes wide and showing the same sort of mild interest as if she'd just asked his opinion of the latest hit movie.

She didn't look like an alien. But this madcap idea of hers belonged to an entirely different planet than the one he lived on.

A husband...that's another thing entirely...

She'd actually asked for his opinion, he reminded himself. *"Amos—darling—what do you think?"* she had said. So he had not only the right but the obligation to answer.

Of course, if he told her what he thought, she'd probably try to have him arrested for using indecent language in the presence of a lady. And she'd be right—at least about the indecent language. As for the part about the lady, that was open to debate.

"What kind of a lady..." He stopped to clear his throat and started over. His voice felt rough. "A lady doesn't propose marriage to a perfect stranger."

Her lovely face went blank for an instant, and then as understanding dawned, her eyes brimmed with horror. "You thought I was suggesting I wanted to marry *you?*"

Now his head was really spinning. *Amos—darling*... But if that wasn't what she'd meant, where had he gone wrong? "It sure sounded that way to me."

"Then you're hearing-impaired as well as arrogant. All I said was—"

"All right, all right. I get it." He gave an exaggerated sigh. "And boy, is that a relief." *You bet it is.*

"How could I be proposing to you? I don't even know your last name."

Amos didn't enlighten her. It wasn't like she was asking for a formal introduction, anyway. "So whom are you planning to marry? Take it from the top and tell me what all this is about. Unless, of course, you're really just talking to yourself and so I'm not supposed to ask."

He thought for a moment that she wasn't going to answer. Then she raised the pointed little chin which was such a distinctive part of every Ladylove ad and said, "It's a business matter."

Either he was getting used to her, Amos thought, or he was growing numb, because he wasn't even vaguely surprised.

She shrugged out of her trench coat, settled back in the chair and took a deep breath.

Amos had been noting the cut of her suit jacket, but he couldn't help being distracted by what the deep breath did to her figure. The Ladylove ads always focused on her face, and the other day when she'd come through the lobby she'd been wearing a coat, ready to go out for the day. So he'd never had an opportunity to pay much attention to the rest of her. But in fact, the shape of her body was very nearly as perfect as the planes of her face. Too bad the quality of her insides didn't match...

"There's this firm I'm trying to buy, you see," she began. "Up until a couple of years ago, Ladylove was totally focused on cosmetics, things like lipstick and eye shadow and foundation and mascara. Then we expanded into perfumes—''

''Courtesy of Denby Miles's formulas,'' Amos mused.

''I see you read the tabloids.'' Her voice was chilly.

''Only while I'm standing in line at the market to buy cat food for Mrs. Haines's Persian on the fourth floor. It was a very slow line this morning.''

''Be glad she didn't send you fishing so Fluffy's lunch would really be fresh.''

''I'll keep that in mind next time she needs to lay in a supply of kibble.''

She crossed her legs.

Nice, long slim legs, Amos noted, with shapely knees that barely peeked out under the hem of a blue wool suit. She must have noticed him looking, because she cleared her throat firmly. She did not, however, make a coy show of pulling her skirt down. Amos liked that.

He sat up a little straighter. ''You were talking about the tabloids.''

''Only because I can't avoid the subject. I'm sure I don't have to explain that the Denby Miles episode didn't happen quite the way the *Sentinel* would like to believe it did.''

I'd give a pretty penny to hear what really did happen.

''At any rate, now Ladylove is ready to expand further, and there's a firm which would be a perfect match.'' She looked at him warily for a long moment, and then seemed to make up her mind to trust him. ''I want to pick up Kate La Croix's line of hair care products.''

Amos frowned. ''I thought Kate La Croix died.''

''She did—about six months ago. That's why her husband wants to sell the business.''

''And since you want to buy, it's a great deal all the way around.''

"Exactly. We can combine two fairly small firms and create a major player."

"Makes sense. I just don't see where the part about the husband comes in. Unless...Oh, now I get it. It's just dawned on you that if you married him instead, you could get the company cheaper."

From her always-placid photographs in the Ladylove ads, Amos thought, one would never suspect that Erika Forrester possessed a temper. Only now did he realize how misleading that impression was. She didn't blow up; he'd give her that. But her gaze was so cold that he found himself feeling a little frosty around the edges.

"That," she said, "is exactly what the kind of idiot who gets his news from the tabloids would think."

"Well, excuse me for being an idiot," Amos said coolly, "but I still don't quite see the problem."

She had the grace to color. "Sorry. I didn't intend that personally. I meant you're not the only one who'll jump to that conclusion."

The phone rang on the desk.

Erika looked at it and then at him. "Aren't you going to answer that?"

"No, I'm going to let voice-mail take it." Amos sliced his sandwich into chunks. "The quicker the tenants learn to share and take turns, the easier it'll be on all of us." The phone rang four times and stopped, and he held out a piece of the sandwich to her.

Erika took it almost absently and nibbled at a corner.

"You were talking about what the tabloids will say," he prompted. "Because of the Denby Miles thing, of course."

"Yes. Half the world thinks I only dated him for those formulas, and that I dropped him the instant my father got his hands on them. Now they're going to think I'm doing the same with Felix La Croix."

"Ignore them. They're tabloids. What difference does it make what they think?"

"It doesn't matter to me—other than being generally annoying. But it matters a great deal to Felix." She pulled a folded paper out of her coat pocket and held it out.

Amos took it reluctantly. The words had obviously been written in haste; the penmanship was uneven, and the signature was nothing more than scrawled initials.

I'm sure you understand why I didn't wish to be part of the show. I'll be in touch when I've had a chance to think things through.

He lifted an eyebrow at her.

She said, sounding reluctant, "That's from Felix. Denby made quite a scene at the Civic Club today."

"And Felix saw it and ducked for cover?"

She nodded. "I can't blame him, exactly. The tabloids haven't heard about the negotiations yet—but they will, and probably soon. There will be a feeding frenzy, and poor Felix will be caught in the middle of speculation about why he's seeing me and what the terms of the sale will be and how long it will take after the agreement's made before I dump him. For a man who's still grieving his wife—"

"That would be a little hard to take," Amos said thoughtfully. "But maybe it'll be an incentive for him to make a quick sale."

"More likely he'll refuse to talk at all, especially if he thinks I'm manipulating the publicity to get him to agree to a fast deal. Which I'm not. But if I was married... settled...obviously not interested in him personally..."

"And you think getting married in order to deflect the tabloids doesn't count as manipulating the publicity? Never mind. If Felix's sensitive feelings are a problem, why not just look for another shampoo company?"

"There isn't another one. Do you think I haven't looked? Most of them are divisions of huge companies, but we couldn't swallow a giant like that even if it was for sale. And Kate's product meshes well with Ladylove's—she insisted on entirely organic ingredients instead of chemical substitutes. Do you know how many shampoos are really just laundry detergent with a nicer smell?"

"Hadn't given it a lot of thought," Amos said. "But it sounds to me like Felix needs you more than you need him. Since it was his wife's company, it must be losing value with every day that goes by. Sit back and wait, and he'll come around."

She shook her head. "No. In fact, sales have gone up since Kate's death—it's actually become sort of a cult thing to use Kate La Croix shampoo. Felix only wants to sell because it's too painful for him to face the reminders every day. I've assured him that we'll keep Kate's name and the brand label. It's a perfect match—if the tabloids will just leave the personal stuff out of it. Which of course they won't, because they've created this image of me."

"So you're thinking of changing the image. Okay," he conceded. "I see where you're coming from. I still think it's a really loopy idea, but let that go for a minute. Who on earth are you thinking about marrying? If you can't even get a date for a Saturday night banquet—"

Her eyes flared. "I have no shortage of dates."

"Then why were you asking Stephen to find you an escort? If you have so many guys standing in line, why not choose one of them rather than add another to the list?"

"Because if I'm seen twice with any one man, the whole gossip mill goes into overdrive."

"And the man in question screams and runs?"

"Or starts bragging that he owns me."

"Well, either variety doesn't offer much promise in the

husband sweepstakes,'' Amos pointed out. He handed her another section of his sandwich.

"What I really need is someone like…'' She looked thoughtful, and then said with a note of triumph, "Someone like Stephen.''

Amos bit his lip hard, but it didn't help much. "Ms. Forrester, I hate to be the one to break the news to you, but Stephen is … Well, let's just say he's not interested in women except as friends.''

She fixed him with a glare. "You think I didn't know that? What difference does it make, anyway? I'm talking about a legal convenience here, not a—'' She broke off.

He couldn't help himself. "Stud service?''

"If that was all I wanted,'' she said bitterly, "I could take my choice.''

He didn't doubt it—and he didn't wonder at her tone, because the reason for her disillusionment was obvious. With her face, her figure and her fame, there must be men aplenty who would happily oblige her in bed—and then brag in the locker room that they'd been with Erika Forrester. She was a trophy. A conquest to boast about.

Hey, he told himself, *don't waste your sympathy. She's the one who's asking for the attention by putting herself in the magazine ads month after month.*

"Well, what you want may not be the most important consideration here,'' he said. "It's the public's perception that counts. So if you want to make everyone believe it's a real marriage, then Stephen's the worst possible choice you could make. Nobody would believe that he's changed, so you might as well not waste your time.''

"Someone like Stephen, then.'' She sounded stubborn. "Someone who's gentle, who's helpful—''

"Someone who owes you,'' Amos put in.

She looked genuinely puzzled. "Why do you say that?''

"Because you can't take a chance on him ruining everything by talking. So unless you can think of someone who'd do it for love—"

She turned a shade paler. "I don't believe in love."

"Well, at least you've got that much sense. I'd hate to think you'd believe it if someone was to conveniently stroll up right now and announce that he was head over heels about you."

"I'd have to be a fool to bite on that one. I'd much rather have a clear-cut business arrangement."

"Then we're back to finding someone who owes you."

She was silent.

"Since you're not rattling off names, that must mean there's nobody already in that category," Amos guessed. "All right, then you'll have to buy him."

"Do you have to be crude?"

"That's not crude, honey, that's just straightforward. You said you wanted it clear-cut. But if you'd rather, we'll call it finding the proper incentives. The bottom line is, what's in it for the guy?"

"There would be benefits," she said stiffly.

"Name two." In the silence that followed, Amos finished the last bite of his sandwich. He picked up a stray crumb, tossed the wrapper in the wastebasket and said, "That's what I thought. You can't."

"Of course I can't be specific," she said stubbornly. "It would depend on the man. Not everyone will be intrigued by the same sort of—"

"Bribe."

"*Benefit.* Anyway, it's not like I'm talking about forever here. This is a short-term bargain. Once the buyout is over, that's it. A couple of months, maybe."

"What happens the next time you want to acquire a company?"

"Look, I don't want to own the world. If I can get this deal through, I'll be satisfied."

"That's what you think now."

"All right," she admitted. "Maybe I will want to buy something else someday. But the circumstances will be different—the seller might even enjoy the gossip. In any case, I'll deal with that later."

"Well, I suppose you could write the marriage contract with a renewal clause," Amos mused. "Sort of like the way that Hollywood options an actor for the sequel when they make the first movie. Which makes a twisted kind of sense, considering this is about as big a special-effects production as we're likely to see around here this year."

"You really think this is ridiculous."

"Since you're asking... Yes."

"I can't thank you enough, Amos darling." She stood up. "You've been so helpful in clarifying my thinking. I'll be sure to let you know what I decide."

"Please do," he said cordially. The phone rang again, and he put a hand on it. "Because I can't wait to hear what happens next."

He was without a doubt right, Erika concluded, when she'd had a chance to think about it. She'd been shaken up by Denby's attack and by Felix's reaction, and she'd gone overboard. It *was* a loopy idea, and not worth further consideration.

Of course, she had no intention of admitting to *Amos darling* that his opinion had influenced her decision. And there hadn't been any opportunity, anyway. In the couple of days since their discussion, she'd seen him only a few times. Even then, she'd spotted him only from a distance, or he'd been tied up with other tenants, or Stephen had been present.

She would just forget the whole thing. She'd continue to ignore the tabloids, Felix La Croix would think it over and get in touch as he'd promised, and they'd make a deal. End of problem.

What she couldn't quite understand was why, since she'd given it up as a loopy idea, she found herself assessing every man who crossed her path, looking at his potential as a husband.

The ad executive who was already working on next spring's campaign was too slick, too flirtatious, too familiar. Ladylove's marketing manager was too serious, too reverential, too much in awe of the boss. The lawyer who was drawing up a tentative contract to offer Felix La Croix was too brash, too arrogant, too presumptuous.

But when on Friday at lunchtime she found herself actually taking stock of the delivery boy who'd brought her Chinese takeout—*too young, too sincere, too ingenuous*—Erika put her face down in her hands and told herself to stop being ridiculous.

Kelly put her head in from the office next door. "Are you all right?"

"No." Erika caught herself. "Yes, I'm fine. Have some Chinese. I'm not hungry anymore."

Kelly pulled up a chair and reached for a set of chopsticks. "You need to eat. You have a photo shoot next week for the fall ads, and you can't look like a skeleton."

"I can't? I thought the ad people preferred me that way."

"No, you can't," Kelly said firmly, "because makeup for dead people doesn't form enough of the market share to keep the company afloat."

Erika wasn't listening. She looked at the draft of the purchase contract she'd been reading when her lunch arrived. "Has Felix La Croix called yet?"

"Not since you asked ten minutes ago."

"He said he'd think it over and get in touch. I've got a meeting with the attorneys in an hour, and I don't have any idea whether we're going to have a deal or not."

Kelly shrugged. "Maybe he's still thinking it over. Or maybe he's hoping if he holds out, you'll sweeten the offer. Maybe you should invite him to take you to the banquet tomorrow...Or have you already decided who to take?"

Erika wanted to groan. "No, and I doubt Felix would be interested. It's only been six months since Kate died."

"Which means it's past time for him to come out of his shell—at least far enough to be sociable. You'd be asking him to take you to dinner, Erika, not meet you at the altar. Right?"

Erika wanted to bang her head on the desk. *Not you, too, Kelly.*

"Anyway, if you're so sure he'll say no, then it's a perfect opportunity to call him. You can get a feel for where he's standing without actually asking whether he's made a decision on selling the business. And that way you won't be stuck with him for a whole evening, either."

"Maybe I'll just take you instead," Erika threatened. "Why should going to an event like this have to look like a date, anyway?"

"Sorry, but I'm already committed. I volunteered to work at one of the publisher's booths—it's a great way to meet people." She reached for the telephone.

Startled, Erika saw that though it hadn't rung, a light was blinking. Line three—her private line. The number she'd given Felix La Croix. Her heartbeat speeded up.

"Ms. Forrester's office," Kelly said. "No, Mr. La Croix, this is her personal assistant. I'll put you straight through." She pushed the hold button and handed the phone to Erika. "Want me to go away?"

Erika shook her head and cleared her throat. "Hello, Felix. I'm sorry we couldn't manage lunch the other day. Perhaps sometime this week?"

He didn't bother to answer. "I was just chased down by a reporter from the *Sentinel.*"

"I'm sorry to hear that." *Not surprised, but definitely sorry.*

"She seemed to think that you and I have some sort of understanding."

Erika allowed a smile to creep into her voice. "I was hoping to hear that myself. About the sale, I mean."

"That's not the sort of understanding she meant. She hinted that the *Sentinel* is ready to run a story that we're planning a wedding."

That's even worse than I expected. "So if they do, they'll embarrass themselves," she said. "It wouldn't be the first time they've been wrong, and it won't be the last."

Felix's voice was firm. "I will not stand for speculation in the public press about my personal life, or gossip that reflects badly on my wife. I'm calling to tell you that I'm starting negotiations with one of your competitors."

Erika's throat tightened till she could hardly breathe. "Felix, you told me you didn't want to sell Kate's company to one of the giants. That was why you were willing to talk to me in the first place."

"Well, conditions change, don't they? I don't see that I have much choice. Unless you can do something to stop this gossip, I will put an end to it by selling the business— to anyone besides you."

Erika swallowed hard. "Give me a few days, Felix. Let me see what I can do."

He didn't answer for a while, and when he did there was a grudging note in his voice. "It's almost the weekend," he said. "All right. I'll hold off till Monday." The telephone banged in her ear.

Big of him to give me a whole weekend. Erika sat frozen.

"That didn't seem to go at all well," Kelly mused.

Erika put the phone down and pushed her chair back. "I think I'll go home early, Kelly."

"What about your appointment with the attorneys?"

"Tell them what happened, and cancel the meeting."

She was almost at the door when Kelly said plaintively, "If you want me to explain it, then don't you think you'd better tell *me* what happened?"

Maybe it was time to just let it go, Erika thought. The few days that Felix had agreed to wait wouldn't make much difference. Perhaps it would be best for her to accept that the deal was not going to go through and turn her attention to something else.

You should have known you couldn't make it work, her father's voice taunted in the back of her mind.

Erika smothered the voice of doubt. She was right about Kate La Croix's products, and she knew it. This was the perfect combination—for Felix La Croix as well as for Ladylove. Why he couldn't see that was beyond her, but obviously he couldn't—so if the deal was to be saved, it would be up to her.

Unless you can do something to stop this gossip…

Well, there was something she could do, Erika told herself. She could undercut the *Sentinel* by making her own announcement first. If she announced her engagement before the *Sentinel* could run its story about her and Felix…

The plan was simple enough in principle. It was the details which weren't so easily settled. What was it Amos had said? *"Who on earth are you thinking about marrying? If you can't even get a date for a Saturday night banquet—"*

There were plenty of possibilities, she told herself. Not the delivery boy from the Chinese restaurant, of course. But the ad manager...the marketing director...the lawyer...

Her brain seemed to grind to a halt. The truth was, she couldn't even imagine herself telling any of them about this scheme, much less asking for their cooperation.

She did have to give *Amos darling* some credit, she admitted. Even though he'd thought the idea was insane, he'd at least listened to her. He'd been helpful at sorting out her thinking once, and maybe he could do that again.

With hope once more rising in her heart, she headed for home.

Amos was in the office when she came in. He was holding the phone between his shoulder and his ear, but he was obviously on hold, because he was sorting notes and reminders on the ever-present clipboard.

"I need to talk to you," Erika announced.

"Take a number. You're about twenty-fifth on the list at the moment."

"I'll wait." She took off her coat, and was startled when Stephen stepped up to take it from her. "I didn't realize you were here, Stephen."

"I just came in," Stephen said. "But before I get started on the list, I'll be happy to take care of your needs, Ms. Forrester."

Erika regarded him thoughtfully. "No, that's all right. Amos has been teaching me to share and take turns, so I'll wait for him to be free."

"Not you, too," Amos muttered.

"What's the matter?" Erika settled into the wing chair. "Is the job more demanding than you expected it to be?

You know, I've been thinking that you looked a little more frazzled every time I've seen you lately.''

Amos shot her a look that should have made her skin sizzle. ''You sound pleased with yourself. You know, I wouldn't put it past you to be getting all the women in the complex to call me every twenty minutes.''

''Why would I do that?'' Erika asked reasonably. ''It just puts me further down your list. Have you had a lunch break yet?''

''Why?'' Amos sounded suspicious.

''Because I'll buy. I owe you from the other day when you shared your lunch and I forgot to even say thanks.''

''And also because that way you can jump to the head of the line.''

''Guilty,'' she admitted.

''I'll take over,'' Stephen said, and reached for the telephone. ''Go.''

Amos stood up, looking reluctant.

Erika reached for her coat. ''How's the book going?''

''You really know how to hurt a guy, don't you?''

''He says,'' Stephen put in helpfully, ''that at this rate he'll finish in about forty-five years.''

''Well, at least that way you don't have to deal with the fear of rejection,'' Erika mused. ''Where would you like to go for lunch?''

Amos guided her out onto the street. ''No place where anyone knows you, that's sure. Which leaves the open-air hot dog stands and the bars.''

''I'll take a hot dog stand. So it's the women who are calling for help? I can't say I'm surprised. What have you been doing for them?''

He sighed. ''Shifting furniture. Plugging a new computer together. Getting boxes down off high shelves.''

''That's a good one,'' Erika said. ''It shows off your

muscles. I did warn you, if you remember, that the residents would keep you busy.''

"Once the news wears off, it'll settle down.''

She thought he sounded more hopeful than convinced.

The nearest hot dog stand was across the street from a tiny park. Erika put mustard on her sandwich and led the way to a bench in the sun. The wooden slats felt warm even through her trench coat.

"So what did you want to talk to me about?'' Amos asked.

"You remember that plan we were talking about the other day? I've decided to go through with it.''

He looked wary. "Why are you telling me?''

"Good manners. You said you wanted to know what I decided. Also…'' She let the silence drag out. "Also because I think you're the perfect candidate.''

Amos went so still that for a moment she thought she was sitting next to a statue. "Oh, no. You're not dragging me into this stunt.''

"I have no intention of dragging you. You said yourself that it's a matter of proper incentives. Or, to make it perfectly clear-cut, bribes. So let's talk about it, Amos darling. What will it take to buy you?''

He didn't answer.

"Forty-five years to write a book,'' Erika mused. "I think maybe there's a way to cut that down. If, of course, you're interested in talking about it.''

CHAPTER THREE

AMOS said, "I can't believe I'm listening to this."

Erika thought he sounded as if he was talking to himself. Or, rather, as if he were lecturing himself. "Why shouldn't you listen?" she challenged. "Because you're afraid if you hear me out you'll be tempted?"

He raised both eyebrows at her. "Wishful thinking, sweetheart."

Erika took a deep breath and regrouped. "Amos, you seem to be a sensible, pragmatic kind of guy. So—"

"Oh, that's great. You know me so well after— What's it been now? Four days and three conversations?"

"You remember exactly?"

"Don't flatter yourself." His voice was heavy with irony. "Of course, with such extensive experience to draw on, you're the expert on what kind of pigeonhole I fit into."

"Don't try to make this about me, Amos. It's not like I don't have reason to think that you keep your own self-interests right at the top of the list. That's why you took this job in the first place, isn't it? It's not exactly your style to be at people's beck and call."

"I'm sure you'll tell me what my style is, oh great psychologist."

"Being independent," she said. "Being your own boss. But you thought this would be a pushover of a job, didn't you?"

He winced.

"I don't mean that in a bad sense," Erika said hastily. "It must have looked very practical at the time. You

41

thought you'd have a nice place to live right in the middle of the action, enough cash to pay the expenses and a lot of free time to do what you wanted."

He sighed. "You got that much right."

"Of course, it didn't turn out that way. If you had more experience with the kind of people who live in upscale Manhattan apartment complexes, you'd have known that."

His gaze flickered, and suddenly he was looking beyond her, into the park.

Oops. Major mistake. "Sorry," she said. " That sounded really snobbish, didn't it? But I was just stating a fact, really."

"You do have a way of stating facts so they sting like darts, you know."

"Hey, as long as we're talking about throwing darts, you're the one who said I need a keeper. But that's all beside the point. Taking the job was a pragmatic and sensible decision to make at the time, even if it hasn't worked out very well. So now that you know the truth about the job, what's so terrible about looking around for a better deal?"

"What you're offering is not a better deal."

"How do you know? We haven't even talked about it." She took a bite of her hot dog. *Don't be in any hurry,* she told herself. *Dangle the idea in front of him and give him a chance to wonder what he might be missing if he walks away.*

He looked at her again. "You've got a point," he said finally. "I may as well listen."

She'd never had any particular desire to go sports fishing, but now she knew how it felt—she'd managed to set the hook, but landing this shark was still going to be a challenge. She took another bite to give herself a moment to think.

"So what are you offering?" Amos asked.

He's impatient. That's good. "Freedom," she said. "The kind you were looking for when you took this job. A roof over your head, food on the table and no more tenants calling you to move computers or stack boxes. All of which comes down to lots of time to write. Interested?"

"And of course a few teeny-weeny little strings attached."

Erika shrugged. "There will be a certain public presence required. But it's not like you have to dangle from my sleeve all day."

He didn't comment. "So what happened to change your mind?"

She told him about Felix's phone call, and he was silent and thoughtful for a long time.

Finally he mused, "He must be an awfully sensitive kind of guy not to thrust out his chest and brag about his name being linked with yours."

"There's Kate—"

"I know, he's a grieving widower and all. Still, to get so bent out of shape about a little gossip that he'll turn down a good offer for a business... You're sure he's not just trying to raise the price you'll pay?"

"He was pretty clear. End the gossip about him by Monday, or he'll be selling to the competition."

"And you don't want to see that happen."

"Of course I don't. Kate's products are the best—I use the stuff myself. If those formulas get into the hands of one of the giants, there will be no point in us even trying to develop a competitive line."

"Maybe this is just his way of getting out of one deal because he has a better one on the horizon," Amos speculated.

"And he wants me to look like the guilty party, so he doesn't appear to be going back on his word?"

"Something like that. They might be offering him more money than you did."

Erika shook her head. "I don't think so. The giants don't need Kate's formulas. I expect at least one of the companies would pick them up if they were handy and cheap, but they're not going to pay an enormous price to secure a niche in the market. Besides, Felix wants to sell to me, because he knows I'll keep Kate's name and her label, and the giants won't. I just have to make it possible for him to do it."

"By stopping the gossip."

She nodded. "Will you help me, Amos?"

His eyes narrowed. "I wondered how long it would take you to get around to actually asking. Until now you've been making it sound as if you were doing me the favor of the century and asking practically nothing in return."

"Well, I am doing you a big favor," Erika pointed out. "And I'm doing myself one, too, of course. That's the beauty of it—there's no downside, because neither one of us is giving up anything." She darted a sideways look at him. "Unless you consider quitting your job to be a sacrifice, of course."

"So what—exactly—are you proposing?"

She leaned forward and tossed her hot dog wrapper in a nearby trash container. "A short-term marriage of convenience."

"Exactly how short-term?"

"By the time all the paperwork is done and we get through the necessary government approvals, probably two to three months. Luckily there's enough competition in the field that we won't have to go through a full-scale antitrust investigation, but—"

"And then?"

"Then we get a quiet annulment, and it's all done with."

"You make it sound very simple."

"That's because it *is* simple. Think about it, Amos. Two or three months of writing all day, every day... How much of your book could you finish in that time?"

"Depends. How many public functions do you anticipate?"

Erika shrugged. "I don't know. Once a week, maybe. All we need to do is be seen together now and then. If there isn't some sort of special event going on, we can go out for lunch. I'm not talking about any huge commitment of time, that's sure. It's not like we'll be living in each other's pockets."

"Speaking of living arrangements—"

"That's right, you'll lose your apartment when you resign."

"Yes. And then there's the fact that it would look a little odd if you were living on the penthouse floor and I was in the basement."

Erika was startled. "The basement? The staff apartments are in the basement?"

"In the employment contract it's technically referred to as the lower level, but—"

"No wonder you're getting no work done. No daylight, no sunshine, no fresh air... My apartment has three bedrooms, and one of them is already set up as a den. Feel free to rearrange the furniture however you like. There's also a screened-in porch and a balcony with a view of Central Park."

"Heaven on earth," Amos murmured.

She decided not to think too hard about the sarcasm obvious in his tone. "Pretty close, actually. I like it much better than the last place I lived. But you've already been in a lot of the apartments, so you know what they're like.''

"Much nicer than the staff's quarters.''

"I'll bet. I'm sure we can work out the day-to-day details. I have a business to run, so I'm hardly home anyway.''

"And that's the whole deal?''

"Well—mostly. Of course there would have to be an agreement that you will never, ever talk to the press about me.''

"And vice versa," he said idly.

"Don't worry about that. I never willingly discuss anything with the *Sentinel,* even the weather.'' She hesitated. "I mean it, Amos—not *ever.* So... Well, I'd be willing to give you some sort of a stipend...''

"As a reminder not to chatter? That sounds like blackmail on the installment plan.''

"Not at all. It's more like—oh, like a legal retainer.''

His eyebrows went up.

"I expect they'll bother you for a while, so it's only fair if I make it worth your while to put up with it.''

"When you put it that way, how can I refuse?'' It didn't really sound like a question—but it didn't exactly sound like agreement, either.

Erika decided not to push her luck by asking.

"What sort of money are you talking?''

Cutting right to the heart of the matter, aren't we? she thought. Well, that was what she'd wanted, wasn't it?—a straightforward, clear-cut discussion? "I said a stipend,'' she warned. "I didn't promise to make you independently wealthy. But I'm quite aware that you can use the money. I mean, writing a novel is a wonderful thing, but it takes time—and anyway, you can't count on getting rich and famous just because there's a dust jacket that has your name on it." She paused. "This is a little embarrassing to ask, but—"

"You amaze me. Erika Forrester, embarrassed—I can't wait to find out why."

"Well…What's your last name, Amos? You never did tell me."

"You never asked," he reminded. "It's Abernathy. Maybe I should write it on your wrist, under your watch-band, so you won't forget it. But then perhaps it doesn't matter since I can't imagine you wanting to use it yourself. And here I thought you were going to ask some really in-timate kinds of questions—like whether I was already mar-ried, or if I have a criminal record."

"Oh." She was speechless for a moment. "Well, I guess I just assumed Stephen would have gone into all that when he hired you. I mean, he did check your references, didn't he? We can't have just anybody running in and out of all the apartments."

Amos started to laugh. "You're priceless, you know that? You're right about the criminal record—and no, I don't have one, unless you count a parking ticket here and there. But as a matter of fact, Stephen never once indicated an interest in whether I was married."

And Amos wasn't about to make it easy on her and vol-unteer the information, either, that was obvious. Erika grit-ted her teeth. "All right. I'll bite. Are you married? Have you ever been married? Are you free to get married? How many ways do you want me to ask it?"

"That'll do. I am without marital entanglements."

"That's good. So—we'll draw up a prenuptial contract just to keep everything tidy, and—"

Amos shook his head. "Nope."

Erika was stunned. He'd agreed…hadn't he? "Did I miss

something here? You can't be refusing to sign a prenup. Can you?"

"Very quick of you."

"But why? It's a piece of paper, that's all."

"A piece of paper which can be copied, passed around and read. You can't seriously be thinking of putting this marriage contract into writing."

"Of course I—" She stopped dead as the implications hit her.

"All the terms, the conditions, the once-a-week lunch, the expiration date, the continuing subsidy to keep my mouth shut? That would make a juicy document for the *Sentinel* to get its hands on."

Erika bit her lip. She didn't even want to think about what the lawyers would say about her getting married without a prenuptial agreement. But he did have a point.

"Lawyers," he said. He sounded as if he was explaining something to a kindergartner. "Clerks. Paralegals. Notaries. Typists. Secretaries... Somebody's going to talk."

"You want to do this on nothing more than a handshake?"

"If we can't trust each other to keep an agreement," he said, "then we'd better start over from the beginning. Or, rather, not start over at all." He stood up. "Thanks for the hot dog. It's been the most interesting lunch date I've had in years."

"All right." Erika jumped up and held out her hand. "It's a deal."

He hesitated for an instant, and then he folded her hand into his.

It wasn't the first time he'd touched her—but the other day, when he'd guided her into a chair, had been a whole lot different sort of contact. Suddenly she had the sense that she was putting much more than her hand into his. It seemed as if he was holding her life in his palm.

How perfectly silly of her. It was a business arrangement, that was all. A short-term solution to a short-term problem.

It must be the relief at having it all settled which was making her feel a little light-headed.

He was looking down at her as if he'd never seen her before. She could understand the feeling.

"Nice to meet you, Erika." His voice was deeper than usual, and her name sounded as if he was uncomfortable. But then, it was the first time he'd actually said her name, she realized. It had always been *Ms. Forrester*, before.

"Likewise," she managed to answer. "Oh, Amos darling—there's one last errand before you quit your job. Can you stop at the courthouse and pick up a marriage license?"

Amos had realized that a significant portion of the population of the western world would have a pithy comment or two to make when the word leaked out that Erika Forrester was marrying an unknown. What he hadn't expected was that Stephen would be both the first and the loudest—and that he would still be going on about it a full twenty-four hours after he'd heard the news.

Amos listened with half an ear while he stared into the mirror on the back of the office door, trying to fix a black bow tie that insisted on migrating toward his left shoulder every time he turned his head. When Stephen paused for a breath, Amos said, "I thought you'd be pleased, since it was your idea to get us together in the first place."

"Get you together?" Stephen howled. "I suggested you escort her to this banquet!"

"Yes, and that's exactly what I'm doing."

"If that was all you were doing... Here, you're only

making that knot worse." With two quick moves, Stephen forced the tie into submission.

"I thought you liked her," Amos said.

"I do—as a tenant. It's true she can be a bit imperious—"

"Imperious? Is that what you call her Queen-Victoria-is-not-amused moments? I couldn't decide between high-handed and just plain bossy. Or maybe overbearing is more like it."

"But she's also generous with approval and thanks."

"Really? I hadn't noticed that part," Amos said. "Though if you'd told me she forks over cold cash for a Christmas bonus and provides the occasional little gift to keep the wheels greased—"

Stephen drew himself up tall. "I would never discuss the various ways in which the tenants choose to show their appreciation."

"Particularly not with someone who isn't on the staff anymore. Look, Stephen, I know you expected I'd stick around for a while, and now I'm leaving you in the lurch."

Stephen shrugged. "I handled it just fine before. I can do it again. Anyway, if you think Ms. Forrester is—what was all that you said? Overbearing and bossy? Then why on earth—"

"Why am I marrying her?" Amos studied himself thoughtfully in the mirror. "Do you have a comb around somewhere? I'm amazed you have to ask the reason. All writers have a masochistic streak in their natures."

"If you think that's any answer—" Stephen dug in the desk drawer and handed over a comb. "Keep it, it's an extra."

"Thanks." Amos used the comb and tucked it into his breast pocket. "Remind me of that favor when it's time for your Christmas bonus."

"Christmas is eight months off. I thought this was a short-term thing."

"It is. I expect to be gone by the Fourth of July. But since I'm a writer, not an actor, I have to try harder to get into the part."

"You need your head examined, Amos. Hanging around here playing manager for a few months is one thing, but this stunt—"

"What's the difference? I'll just be hanging out upstairs instead of in the lobby. See you, buddy."

He took the elevator to the penthouse floor. Perhaps, he thought idly, he should have pressed Stephen a little harder about the reasons he was so upset about this deal. If there was something Stephen knew about Erika...

Of course, if it was anything to her discredit, the *Sentinel* would have published it long ago, Amos reflected. Unless only Stephen knew it. Maybe she kept whips and chains in her apartment....

He noticed when she answered the door that she seemed shorter than usual. But that was because she wasn't wearing shoes, he saw. Beneath the hem of the tightly wrapped dark blue dressing gown, her slender feet were bare, the toes curling against the obviously cold white marble floor of the entry.

"Sorry," she said. "I'm running a little late. Come in and make yourself a drink while I put my dress on."

"Spoken in a true wifely manner," he mused. "A mistress, on the other hand, would suggest making myself a drink while you took your dress off."

"Now there's a useful distinction." She pointed, past a pair of sleek pillars which separated the entry from the living room, toward a bar tucked into the far corner. Then she padded away, her feet nearly silent against the stone. The room she entered was almost directly across the hall from the bar, and though she gave the door a push as she went through, it didn't quite shut behind her.

Amos looked at the door with a frown. It was odd, he thought, that she'd barely reacted to that wisecrack about not yet being dressed. And odder still that she hadn't made a point of firmly closing—maybe even locking—her bedroom door.

Though when he considered it further, he decided that maybe it wasn't odd at all. The woman was a model—she might have gotten so used to being poked, prodded and treated like an object that she no longer felt shy at being half-dressed in front of strangers. Or perhaps she'd planned this very deliberately, to test him—figuring that if he took a half-open door as an invitation to follow her, she could hit him with a can of Mace and back out of the whole plan.

As if he had no more self-control than that. As if he was even interested. So what if she was gorgeous by conventional standards? There was a lot more to true beauty than wide-set violet eyes in an almost triangular face. More than a slim, lithe body which was just the right size to be an armful...

It dawned on him that he was still standing right inside the door, exactly where he'd been when she walked away, and he headed toward the bar. A slug of Scotch sounded good, all of a sudden. "Want me to make you something?" he called across the hallway.

"A sherry, maybe."

He'd half expected that she would have gone on into a bath or dressing room and might not be able to hear him at all. But her voice was only slightly muted. Which meant she must have stopped just inside the room to take off the robe...to lift her dress carefully over her already arranged hair...to struggle to reach the zipper...

He spotted the sherry bottle and got down a small

stemmed glass from a shelf. "Wise choice—asking for something I can't mess up. Stephen hadn't gotten around to starting my bartending lessons yet."

"Really? I thought all great writers had been bartenders—that it was in the blood."

"Maybe I'll try it after this gig's over."

The bedroom door opened. He was startled by the tap of high heels on marble, because he hadn't expected her to reappear for a good twenty minutes.

Her dress was made of some soft stuff that looked like it had been spun from a cloud, shot through with silvery threads that caught the light. It had long sleeves but no shoulders at all—how they'd hooked the thing together was an engineering feat worthy of a prize, in Amos's opinion—and not much of a skirt.

He was certain there was a name for the color, but it was one he'd never seen before outside of a sunset. It was definitely not pink, but it sure wasn't purple, either. Just a little lighter than her eyes, it made them look like enormous, mysterious, deep pools.

She didn't pose and she didn't fish for compliments. And a good thing, too, Amos thought. What would he have told her? That it looked to him like the designer had started out with a good idea but run out of fabric long before he was done?

Her gaze flicked across him as she reached for the sherry glass. "Nice tux."

"Of course it is. Stephen arranged the rental."

She smiled. "Hey, you're getting into the swing of this already—realizing how nice it is to have a Stephen to call on... You should probably buy your own tux, though. It won't be any more expensive than renting, and then you'll have it for afterward."

"And I'd need it for...?"

"All the bashes to honor you when your book comes out."

"Of course. I thought maybe you meant I could wear it for my next wedding."

She didn't hesitate. "That, too. You never know when it will come in handy. As long as we're speaking of your book—"

"We are?"

"I want to do everything I can to help you be successful, Amos. But I need to know a little more about the book, because it will make a difference in how I introduce you."

"*My fiancé* isn't a good enough label?"

"Amos, there will be publishers there tonight. Agents. Editors. I know these people. When they find out you're with me, they'll bend over backward to help. If I introduce you as *my fiancé who's writing the greatest American novel of the twenty-first century, the Huck Finn of its day*—"

Amos shook his head. "Not even close."

"Well, that's refreshing." She set the half-full sherry glass aside. "I've never before met an author who didn't think his work was the product of genius."

"I didn't say I'm not a genius," he said modestly. "Just that my book's not remotely like Huck Finn."

It was the first time he'd seen her react with genuine delight. She gave a little gurgle of laughter, and her smile gave her eyes the rich glow of amethysts and made an already arresting face even more heart-stoppingly lovely.

They should put that smile in the ads, he thought. Except that if they did, Ladylove would probably get sued for being unfair to the competition.

Erika checked her cape in the women's cloakroom right outside the hotel's grand ballroom and went on into the lounge to be sure her makeup hadn't picked up a speck on the taxi ride downtown. To her surprise, Kelly was there, fussing with her hair.

"You're just getting here?" Erika asked. "I thought you were volunteering."

"I have been. I'm just freshening up after a couple of hours of unpacking books and putting one at every place setting."

"Table favors?"

"Courtesy of the publishers. Reserve your chair quickly enough, and you can choose which title you get to take home. But I'd chewed off all my lipstick while I tried to get just the right mix of mystery and horror and romance and sci-fi at each table, so I'm taking a break."

"Sounds like a well-deserved one. Kelly—could you use a bonus?"

"Extra money? Always, as long as the job's not unethical or illegal, and it doesn't cause me to sweat."

"Do me a favor." Erika pulled out her makeup kit and touched up her mascara. "Go call the *Sentinel* and tell them I'm here tonight with my fiancé."

"You want me to make an announcement that you're *what?*"

"No announcement. Nothing formal, because they'd think it was a setup. You're calling in an anonymous tip, just because you thought they'd like to know that you heard me introduce my fiancé."

"And they won't think that's a setup? Erika, if you believe that kind of tall tale's going to stop them from linking you with Felix—"

Erika pulled a handful of coins from her evening bag. "Here. There's a pay phone by the cloakroom."

"I'll get the giggles," Kelly protested. "What are you thinking?"

"That I'd better get into the ballroom and introduce my fiancé before the *Sentinel* gets here."

Kelly trailed her to the door. "If you're engaged, Erika, where's the rock?"

Erika stopped dead in the hallway. A ring. She'd forgotten all about an engagement ring.

"It's...um...being reset at the jewelers," she said. "The stone was in my fiancé's family, but the setting was worn-out."

Kelly smirked. "Right. So what are you *really* up to?"

"Here he is now," Erika said. Amos was waiting by the ballroom door. She laid a hand on his arm, raised onto her tiptoes, and lightly kissed his cheek. "Kelly, this is my fiancé. Amos darling, Kelly's my personal assistant. You'll no doubt see a lot of her."

Kelly goggled at her. Then she turned to look at Amos, and her eyes widened even more.

"The wedding's Tuesday," Erika added blandly. "We'll have a lot to do on Monday to get ready for it, of course—but do have a relaxing weekend in the meantime. Let's go on in and choose our seats, darling. Shall we save you one, Kelly, since you'll be delayed by that phone call you need to make?"

Kelly shook her head, almost in slow motion, as if she couldn't believe what she was seeing.

Erika drew Amos toward the ballroom door. "We'll have to do something about a ring tomorrow. Nobody thinks an engagement is official unless there's a diamond. In the meantime, if anyone asks, just tell them you're having a family stone reset for me."

"I'm glad you were clear about wanting a diamond," he said dryly. "Where I'm from, a family stone is more likely to refer to marble or granite. What's this about a phone call?"

"Just keep an eye out for people with cameras. They'll be here shortly."

"And what do I do if I see one?"

She was scanning the crowd already gathered inside the ballroom. "A mild public display of affection would be appropriate."

"Perhaps we should define the term before the need actually arises. Does this qualify?" He bent his head and brushed his lips against her nape.

An icy little thrill ran down Erika's spine.

"How about this?" He nibbled her earlobe. "Or perhaps this?" His fingertips pressed against her bare shoulder blade, five tiny hot spots which urged her closer to him. With his other hand, he nudged her chin up until her lips were almost against his.

Erika was finding it hard to breathe. "All right," she managed to say. "You've escalated far enough."

"What a disappointment. I thought perhaps we could just slide under the table during the after-dinner speeches." He let her go and tucked her hand into the bend of his arm to lead her further into the ballroom.

Booths down one entire side of the room boasted the familiar logos of publishers and bookstores. There were huge posters, piles of books and people milling around or already sitting at the round banquet tables. Other chairs were obviously already claimed, occupied by bags or jackets while their owners socialized.

Just yards away, a short round woman with improbably black hair and a bright green dress looked up from a rack of bestsellers and spotted Erika. She dodged through the crowd toward them.

Erika smothered a sigh and tried to encourage herself. *It's all in a good cause. And fortunately, tonight I have a distraction to offer her.* "Hello, Phillippa. You're looking well."

"You've been dodging me, you naughty girl." Phillippa's voice was deep and rough, the mark of a long-term smoker. She loudly kissed the air beside Erika's cheek. "And you've been thinking about my offer, I hope."

"Oh, of course."

"It's still good, you know. Yours is a great story, and we could sell it to any of these publishers." She waved a hand which took in every booth in sight. "I'd love to auction it tonight."

And turn a mere fund-raiser into a circus. "Oh, let's deal with my business some other time." *Like well after the moon dwindles entirely to dust particles.* "There's someone I would like you to meet, Phillippa. This is Amos Abernathy. He's an author. Amos darling, Phillippa Strang. She's an agent."

Phillippa's eyes narrowed. "I don't recognize the name. Who represents you?"

"Oh, you wouldn't have heard it before." Amos stretched out a hand. "I'm a complete unknown."

Phillippa ran an appraising eye over him. "Well, in that case, we need to get the terminology straight. Until someone is actually published, he's not an author—just a writer."

"I'll remember that," Amos said.

Erika shot a look at him. He'd sounded meek—which was enough to raise her suspicions instantly. But he seemed to be completely sincere.

Phillippa's gaze was still glued to Amos, as if she was trying to memorize his face. "Well, it's an easy enough mistake to make," she allowed. "If you do anything in my field, I'd like to look at your stuff."

I'll bet you would, Erika thought. *Only I don't think the stuff you're talking about has anything to do with writing.*

"That's very kind of you, Ms. Strang."

"Oh, let's start off as friends. Call me Phillippa."

"Sweetheart," Amos murmured into Erika's ear, "you're so right—people are bending over backward to be helpful tonight."

"Sweetheart?" Phillippa's gaze had sharpened and was veering back and forth between Amos and Erika.

"Yes, Amos is also—besides being a very good *writer*—my fiancé," Erika said sweetly. "Oh, look, darling, there are two seats left over there in the corner. The tables are filling up fast. I think we'd better grab them, don't you?" She smiled at Phillippa and steered Amos away.

"You want to tell me what that was all about?" Amos asked. "Why did you introduce me if you didn't want her to talk business?"

Erika glanced around the table. Of the ten seats, five were occupied, two were tipped up against the table and obviously reserved and another was swathed in a mink stole left to mark the spot. "Are these last two seats taken? No? Thank you."

Amos held a chair for her.

She said, almost under her breath, "Is that what you call *talking business?* I don't think bending over backward was quite the position she was thinking about getting into with you."

Amos smiled. "Very good, my dear."

"What do you mean?"

He leaned closer, his arm resting along the back of her chair, so it cradled her shoulders, his mouth almost touching her ear. "I was complimenting your public display of affection. It's just too bad there wasn't a photographer

handy right then—but I think the word will spread anyway.'' His breath tickled. ''I must say I wouldn't have
thought of it myself. Very effective, Erika—acting jealous
like that.''

CHAPTER FOUR

JEALOUS? How dare he suggest that she was acting jealous?

Erika was breathless for an instant at the very idea. The last emotion she could possibly feel toward Phillippa Strang was jealousy. Irritation and annoyance, yes—the woman was good at provoking that sort of reaction. But jealousy? And over Amos, of all things—how ridiculous could he get?

Then she saw the humor of it all. If the public wanted to put that interpretation on it, what harm could it do? Amos was right that the word would spread—she couldn't have chosen a better medium than Phillippa to make her announcement. And if Erika herself was seen as being jealous—well, a woman who was displaying signs of the green-eyed monster over one man was hardly going to be suspected of having an extra one on the string. That ought to end speculation about her and Felix in a heartbeat.

She patted Amos's cheek with what she hoped looked like fondness, and turned away to introduce herself to the person at her left.

The noise level in the ballroom was changing—the roar of conversation had died down but was replaced by chairs scraping and carts rumbling as a parade of waiters brought out the first course.

"Better move your book," Amos said as the waiter started around their table with clear soup.

"Book?" Erika remembered what Kelly had said about table favors, and she picked up her napkin to reveal a brightly jacketed hardcover novel lying on the service plate.

61

"*Pulling Up Stakes,* by Madison Adams," she said. "Well, I could be wrong. But judging by the blood-dripping fangs on the cover, I doubt it's a historical novel about a wagon train leaving Missouri to settle the West."

Her neighbor on the left laughed. "I was getting ready to trade," he said, holding up a romance featuring a shirtless pirate with a patch-covered eye. "But then you sat down and I thought it would look rude to grab your book."

A woman across the table told him, "I'll swap with you," and she handed over a collection of sci-fi stories in return for the pirate.

Erika looked at the book which had been part of Amos's table setting. He'd put it off to the far side of his plate, and it was half-hidden under the evening's program of events. But the subject matter was pretty clear from the title, she thought. *With Malice Toward One,* by Judd Thorne. She could see a shadowy shape on the front cover which might be private investigator, villain, or just decoration. "Don't look so disappointed," she said. "It might only be an ordinary murder mystery, but at least you could read it on an airplane without being embarrassed by the art on the cover."

"You can borrow it for your next business trip."

"Thanks. I'll keep that in mind." Erika turned her attention back to her own book, flipping it over to read the back cover copy aloud. "*With its two-month-long night, Stakeout, Alaska, is the winter vacation destination of choice for American vampires, and Jake Wilson's Club Red is their favorite hangout. But when Jake's customers start coming down with fatal blood reactions, the bar is suspected of...*" She wrinkled her nose. "I can't wait to go home, tuck myself in and start reading."

"Someone must like them," Amos said. He pointed at

the back of the dust jacket. "Not only is it hardcover, but look at the list of titles in the series."

"*Stakeout,*" Erika mused. "That must have been the first one, since it's the name of the town, too. *Raising the Stakes, Drawing Blood...* I see what you mean. I guess I'll hang on to it. I'll have a mint copy in case Madison Adams turns out to be the Hemingway of his day. Or, possibly, her day—there doesn't seem to be a picture anywhere. Let me see your mystery."

Amos handed the book to her. The waiter bustled around the table, and their fellow diners began to eat their soup.

Erika looked at the book, read the back cover and shrugged. "It sounds okay to me. Way more interesting than the vampires."

"That wouldn't take much."

"Don't be such a snob, Amos. Reading for fun has its place. Just because you're writing the great American novel—"

For a moment, with everyone else at the table occupied, it seemed as if they were alone for the first time since they'd gotten out of the cab.

Amos said, "Have you been holding out on me?"

"About what?" She gave the book back and picked up her spoon. "I'm not a closet mystery buff, if that's what you mean. And I'm not fascinated by vampires, either. I mostly read corporate reports and business magazines."

"No—I meant what the agent was saying about you having a great story. It sounded like she wants you to write a book."

"Well, next time she brings it up I'll tell her there's room for only one author—I beg your pardon, *writer*—in a family. What she wants, actually, is a tell-all. She says she'll call it something ridiculous like *Growing Up Beautiful,* and it's to be my life story. But what she's really after is an exposé about how my father built his business, all the models and beautiful women he slept with and what it was like to live in his shadow.''

"And you're not going to cooperate."

"Of course not. I lived through it—I'm not about to wallow in the details now.'' She glanced around the room. "There's an editor I know, sitting two tables over—or at least I have a speaking acquaintance with her, if you'd like to be introduced. And there's the marketing manager from one of the publishing houses. They use the same ad agency we do, so I could scrape up a conversation. That might be interesting, finding out how they—''

"Eat your dinner," Amos recommended.

She picked up her soup spoon. "I did say I'd do anything I could to help."

"Helping out doesn't require you to go hungry."

"Trust me, with banquet food that's not a problem. Hungry is better."

But she was wrong about that, for tonight even the food was miles above standard banquet fare. Better yet, the group at the table was unusually chatty, considering that they were total strangers brought together for a single evening only by a common cause.

The way Kelly had scattered books—seemingly at random—had been a brilliant move, Erika thought. Because of the wide variety around the table, everyone had something to talk about. There was even a spirited defense of vampire stories from a couple sitting across from them.

"Now there's a scary thought," Amos whispered in her ear.

"You mean the fact that they already own every Madison Adams title every published?"

"And read them aloud to each other in bed. Makes me wonder what other pastimes they enjoy."

She tried to smother her giggle, without much success.

The man sitting next to the vampire-defenders nodded at the mystery lying beside Amos's dessert plate. "That's actually a pretty good book," he said. "I borrowed it from the library when it first came out—I always do that with new authors, rather than buy an unknown."

"Want to trade?" Amos offered. "You could have your own copy."

The man shook his head. "No, thanks. Now that I know what happens, I don't need to read it again."

"That's an interesting philosophy," someone else offered. "I wonder what a Shakespeare scholar would say about never needing to read something a second time."

The mystery-lover laughed. "Well, Judd Thorne is hardly Shakespeare. Does anyone but me think that an author's first mystery is usually his best?"

"Shush," his wife said. "They're going to introduce the speaker."

"I'd much rather talk about first books," the mystery-lover said unrepentantly.

Amos leaned toward Erika. "There's a determined-looking gentleman approaching from the left. I don't see a camera, but—"

Erika sneaked a glance over her shoulder. All over the room people were moving—some returning to their tables in time for the speeches to begin, others switching chairs to get a better view of the podium, and a few, she was certain, actually sneaking out. Waiters were still circling, picking up used plates and delivering final cups of coffee. In the bustle, it took her a minute to spot the man Amos had noticed.

"That's Felix," she murmured. "I wonder what he wants."

Felix La Croix was now bearing down on her like a man-of-war in full sail. "If I might have a moment, Ms. Forrester," he said, almost without moving his lips.

"Certainly." She looked around at the nearest tables. "There's a chair you can pull over."

But Felix didn't answer, simply marched away toward a row of pillars which separated the main section of the ballroom from the kitchen entrance. He was obviously expecting her to follow. Despite the bustle of the crowd, he was still apparently worried at being seen with her—which was far from a good sign. She laid aside her napkin and stood up.

Amos rose, too.

Erika started to tell him she could handle Felix by herself, and then decided that reinforcements might not be a bad idea after all. What could Felix want, anyway? It could hardly be business, because he'd promised to give her till Monday. He must have heard by now about her and Amos—but if that was what had brought him over, surely he'd have made a show of public congratulations...

Felix had ducked behind the first pillar in the row. "What kind of game are you playing?" he fumed as she joined him. "The first thing I heard when I came in tonight was the rumors about an engagement."

"Rumors about *our* engagement?" Erika asked. "Or about *my* engagement? Because there's a big difference. I'd like to introduce you to—" She half-turned to draw Amos into the conversation, and found herself facing thin air.

He had been no more than a couple of steps behind her as she crossed the room. Though he hadn't been touching her, Erika had known exactly where he was. But now he was nowhere to be found.

She looked around desperately, but it was impossible to see far because the crowd was greeting the speaker with a standing ovation. Still, Amos should have stood out against the masses of people, since he was taller than average. His dark hair and broad shoulders should catch her eye even in a mob...

"I asked you to squash the rumors." Felix was so angry he was practically spitting. "Instead I hear all sorts of speculation. Once and for all, I have no intention of marrying you, so no matter what kind of public pressure you bring to bear—"

Erika was stunned. Felix thought she'd set this up on purpose because she *wanted* to marry him? She opened her mouth to demolish him.

But in the meantime, Amos had reappeared, materializing beside her almost as suddenly as a ghost. "Of course you aren't going to marry her," he told Felix soothingly, before she could speak. "Erika, sweetheart, I hope you realize you have a responsibility for this misunderstanding."

"*I* have a responsibility?" she gasped. *And you have a nerve!*

"Of course. You really must stop treating every man you meet as if he's irresistible, because they start to believe it, and then they begin acting like animals. I'm sorry to interrupt—La Croix, is it?"

"Who asked you to butt into this conversation?" Felix blustered. "Who are you, anyway?"

Amos ignored him. "You were telling me before dinner, darling, that no one considers an engagement official without a ring." With a gesture worthy of a magician, he held out one hand. The velvet box on his palm seemed to have appeared out of thin air. "So let's make it official."

He took her hand and drew her around the pillar and back to the edge of the ballroom, to an area which was less cramped. He dropped to one knee, one hand holding hers, the other displaying the ring box. "Erika, will you marry me?" His voice wasn't loud, but in the momentary silence as the crowd settled into their chairs again and the speaker drew breath to begin, his words rang through the corner of the ballroom.

Erika didn't consciously move, but she must have done something that looked like agreement, for people at the tables nearest them broke into approving sighs, smiles and even applause.

Amos pressed a hidden catch on the box with his thumbnail, and it sprang open. The diamond ring inside caught the lights and reflected straight into Erika's eyes just as a dozen flashes went off in her face. She wasn't sure which was the brightest, just that she was momentarily blinded.

She felt the touch of cool metal and warm skin as Amos—still kneeling—slid the ring onto her finger. Then he tugged lightly at her hand until she took the hint and bent forward till her lips gently brushed his. The flashes went off again.

Amos got to his feet. Everyone in the ballroom was watching, or trying to, Erika saw. He put an arm around her and drew her close.

She couldn't get her breath. It had been difficult enough to stand still and let him almost kiss her earlier, just outside the ballroom when no one had been paying any attention. Now it took all the self-discipline Erika could muster to smile, to let her hand slide up the slick lapel of his jacket to the back of his neck, to look interested, to make a mechanical going-through-the-motions kiss look convincing.

Or, even worse, to submit to a triumphant, possessive kiss—the kind a man might claim when he was showing off, boasting to the world that he was the chosen one. But it was too late to stop him. She'd simply have to let him kiss her, no matter how he chose to do it.

He chose a way she hadn't anticipated at all. His mouth

was soft, gentle, but hot—demanding in an odd sort of way that had nothing to do with force or domination.

And he tasted like chocolate mousse—though Erika had no idea why that should startle her, since she'd watched him eat the dessert just minutes ago.

She closed her eyes, but she could still see the flashes going off. Or were those sparks of light originating inside her brain, caused by his kiss?

She didn't know how long he kissed her, though she had the odd sensation that it was both longer and shorter than any kiss she'd ever experienced before. It was long enough that the paparazzi must have run out of film before he raised his head, but short enough that she found herself wishing he hadn't stopped.

"That should do it," Amos said under his breath.

Erika had to agree that it had been a convincing performance. She, herself, was feeling just a little let down now that it was over. "Where's Felix?"

"He disappeared when the cameras came out. No surprise there." He held their clasped hands above his head as if announcing the winner in a prize fight and called to the speaker, "Sorry about the interruption. We'll behave ourselves and let you have the floor now."

Erika was still feeling dazed as he led her through the laughing crowd back to their table, where eight beaming faces waited. "We had no idea," the female half of vampire-novel couple said. "Let's see your ring, dear."

Erika stole a glance at the diamond herself while the women at the table were admiring it. The central stone was huge, the shape of a teardrop, and so white it almost hurt her eyes. At each side of the platinum mounting was a small amethyst.

The speaker finished a joke, and under the cover of laughter, she whispered, "Amos, where did it come from?"

Amos said blandly, "I don't know."

She frowned. "What are you talking about? It can't have just turned up in your pocket. I thought perhaps you'd borrowed one from someone in the crowd."

"A borrowed ring for my fiancée? Erika, precious, that would be tacky. Besides, it would never have worked, because too many people would recognize it."

"Well, you've barely been out of my sight since I remembered that we'd need a ring. So how did you manage to pull one out of the hat?"

"Just because you forgot doesn't mean I did."

Erika felt as if he'd punched her. "You had it in your pocket all this time? But why hold it back till now?"

"Oh, no, I haven't been carrying it around all evening. I didn't remember it till we got here, so I called Stephen while you were in the lounge talking to Kelly." He glanced at his watch. "It took him long enough to come through. I must admit I was beginning to wonder whether he was going to be able to pull it off at all."

"But where'd he get it?"

"You mean, which jeweler did he talk into opening up shop especially for you? I have no idea." His voice was lighthearted. "I told him to charge it, by the way—so I expect you'll find out in a few days when the bill comes."

Stephen was still in his office when they came into the lobby of the apartment complex. It was unusually late for him to be working, and Erika was fairly sure he'd stayed on purpose but was trying to look as if he hadn't.

"Checking to make sure we'd beat the curfew?" Amos asked him cheerfully. "Or wanting to know whether the diamond was well-received? Your reputation as a miracle worker is secure, buddy." He set the books he was carrying on the desk and leaned against the corner of it.

"Thank you, Stephen," Erika said. "The ring was a life-saver."

"Yes, it was definitely the high point of the evening," Amos said. "The look on Felix's face when he realized that he wasn't the center of attention after all was priceless. In fact, the whole evening was worthwhile just for the pleasure of deflating his ego."

"Though I may end up apologizing to him," Erika mused, "for you saying he was behaving like an animal."

"Why? He didn't even notice he was being insulted."

"I wouldn't be too sure of that, once he gets home and thinks it over."

Amos shook his head. "He was still absorbing the shock of discovering that you didn't prefer him after all."

"We'll see." Erika reached for the books Amos had carried in. "I hope you're right."

Stephen was looking at the covers with astonishment. "Ms. Forrester—"

"It only looks like she's acquiring weird new tastes," Amos put in. "Hard as it is to believe, our Ms. Forrester turns out to be a bargain-hunter. The books were free, so she refused to leave them behind."

"They were hardly free," Erika argued. "I paid five hundred dollars a ticket for that banquet, so I'm certainly not going to turn down the souvenirs. Besides, it would have hurt the organizers' feelings if people had walked off and left their gifts. Good night, both of you."

It didn't dawn on her until she was in the elevator that such a casual farewell was hardly the usual way to say good-night to one's fiancé—the man she'd be marrying in just a couple of days. She'd have to be more careful. They couldn't afford to let too many people know the truth about this, and that too-casual good-night would have been a dead giveaway.

Tonight only Stephen had been in the lobby, and Stephen was safe; she could tell him anything. It wasn't necessary to perform for his benefit. But if there had been other tenants around…

She shivered a little at the thought of repeating that kiss. It was a good thing she hadn't had time to think about it beforehand. It had just…happened. But now that she knew what it was like to kiss Amos…

Fortunately the problem wasn't likely to arise often. Once they were officially married, there would be no need to go around convincing people of their affection. And a good thing, too, she told herself.

She held up her left hand. Even in the subdued, yellowish light of the elevator, the diamond was strikingly beautiful. The size of her smallest fingernail, the stone seemed to glow with its own internal light, drawing her gaze ever deeper into the facets until she realized with a start that the elevator had not only stopped on her own floor but the door had started to close again while she stood there and stared at a rock, oblivious to everything else around her.

She caught the elevator door just in time, went into her living room and flopped down in the nearest chair. The automatic chant in the back of her brain reminded her to sit up straight. *A model never forgets her posture….*

"Well, I haven't forgotten it, Father," she snapped. "I'm just ignoring it for the moment."

It was the first instant she'd had to relax since the banquet. In fact, well before the banquet—she'd been on edge even before Amos had rung the bell.

After that grandstand announcement, however, it had gotten worse. They'd been watched and commented about to such an extent that she'd felt sorry for the poor speaker, who had been facing impossible competition for his audience's attention. And as soon as the evening began to break up, they'd been surrounded by a chattering crowd. Erika felt as exhausted tonight as she always did after a day-long photo shoot.

But now, in the restful silence of her apartment, she could finally actually take her time and reflect on the evening.

Everything had gone pretty well, actually, she thought. Except, of course, for that odd pronouncement of Felix's. What on earth was wrong with him, to think that she was trying to maneuver him into marrying her?

Amos was right that Felix wasn't exactly short on ego. But how he'd gotten the notion that she was serious about him...

She was tempted to call off the whole deal. Who needed that kind of aggravation?

But she did want Kate La Croix's product line. In fact, she needed it. Or at least, she needed to be sure that Kate's formulas didn't get into the hands of her competitors.

And in any case, she reminded herself, she'd committed to Amos. She'd promised him three months in which he could write full-time, expense-free, in return for the sort of help he'd so brilliantly provided tonight. He was living up to his end of the bargain splendidly, so how could she say that she'd changed her mind?

Of course, she could still carry through with almost everything she'd promised. It probably wouldn't make much difference to him whether he was living in her penthouse or somewhere else, as long as he had enough money for rent, food and lights to write by. He might even be relieved to find that it wasn't necessary to go the whole distance after all in order to get his benefits package.

She stared at the teardrop-shaped diamond on her finger, and suddenly she felt like crying.

* * *

The building which housed the headquarters of Ladylove Cosmetics was sleek and modern, but unassuming—the odds that it had ever won an award for architecture were nonexistent. In fact, Amos thought, it looked like a cross between a bath powder box—the kind his mother used to keep on her dressing table—and a perfume bottle, only on a giant scale. The facade was rounded, and the glass block accents at each side of the door reminded him of the facets on an expensive crystal scent spritzer.

He didn't know what to expect. A giant version of the Ladylove kiosks which could be found in every department store, perhaps. He'd walked past one just a few days ago, when he'd gone downtown to pick up that white silk blouse for Erika...

A blouse he'd forgotten to return, he realized. Well, there had been a few other things on his mind.

At any rate, he'd walked past the Ladylove kiosk that day with far more interest than he usually felt. He'd never paid much attention to women's makeup and perfume—not unless some woman was wearing way too much of one or the other in an effort to impress him—but having met the majority owner had given the whole subject a new interest.

Of course then he hadn't realized just how much that interest would grow. He hadn't anticipated ever being invited to visit the company's headquarters.

He'd half expected glass booths, lots of shelves and hundreds of gray and silver boxes full of lipstick and eye shadow. But the lobby of Ladylove's building was sleek and quiet, an expanse of gray carpet broken only by the modern curve of a receptionist's desk, the walls covered by a subtly patterned paneling which looked like aluminum. The only identifying marks were the Ladylove logo on the wall opposite the entrance, and a row of larger-than-life portraits which stretched off to each side of the logo. There were no names—no individual identification. These were the Faces of Ladylove, the gorgeous but always silent women who had, in succession, represented the company.

Many were before his time, though he recognized a few who had gone on to other careers in fashion modeling or acting after leaving Ladylove. Some seemed vaguely familiar from half-remembered ads.

The receptionist looked up, but before he could give his name, she said, "Mr. Abernathy? I'll let Ms. Forrester know you've arrived."

He wondered idly whether she'd had a very good description of him or if there were so few visitors that she knew all the regulars. She picked up the phone, and—feeling dismissed—he wandered over to look more closely at the portrait wall. On the very end was Erika, four times life-size—unsmiling, her violet eyes wide.

"Major mistake," he said under his breath.

The artist must have worked the image over with an airbrush, he thought. No one's complexion could really be so perfect, not at that magnification level. Not that he'd noticed any flaws last night while he was kissing her...

"Mr. Abernathy?"

He wheeled around to face Erika's personal assistant. Kelly looked a little more in her element today, he thought. But then she'd had a couple of days to get used to the idea; he couldn't blame her for looking as if Erika had smacked her in the face Saturday night outside the ballroom. The shock value of a slap probably couldn't have been any greater.

"Call me Amos. Congratulations on bringing the paparazzi out in force the other night. No wonder Erika relies on you."

Kelly shook her head. "Not my doing, really. By the time I got through to someone in charge at the *Sentinel,* the cameras were already swarming. What did you mean about a major mistake?''

He let his gaze drift back to Erika's photograph. "A smile would be better."

"The Face of Ladylove has always been a serious one."

"One could even say somber." He pointed at a portrait halfway down the row, of a woman who was just as blonde, just as beautiful, as Erika was. Her eyelids were painted in the highly colored fashion of her time, but beyond the makeup lay an even darker shadow, an inner pain in her eyes which the dramatic makeup only heightened. "Perhaps it's time for a change."

And perhaps you should keep your opinions to herself. Amos could almost hear Kelly thinking it. And she was probably right, he told himself. What he knew about the cosmetics business would fit in a lipstick tube, and he was no expert on advertising or marketing, either. Besides, the last thing he needed was for Erika to get the idea that he was trying to butt in and tell her how to run her business.

"But that's just me being selfish," he added smoothly. "I prefer to see her smiling, that's all."

Kelly eyed him quizzically. "This way," she said, and led the way to the elevator. "That portrait was of Mrs. Forrester, by the way."

"The very sad woman was Erika's mother?"

"Not at the time the picture was taken, of course. That photograph was made not long after they were married, but she stopped modeling when she became pregnant."

"And then there were other Faces of Ladylove," Amos mused, thinking about the number of portraits in between the ones of mother and daughter.

He wondered how many of them Stanford Forrester III had slept with. From the nonchalant way Erika had referred to her father's love affairs, he'd bet it was most of them.

"Erika would like you to join her in her office until it's time for the ceremony, by the way." Kelly tapped on a door and then closed it behind him.

Amos wondered if this had been Stanford Forrester's office. If so, he'd bet that nothing from that era had survived, for now it was a graceful and feminine room. There were no ruffles, no lace, no frills—but there was absolutely no doubt that this was a woman's space. The Georgian table with its gracefully curved legs almost matched the mantel over the gas-log fireplace along the opposite wall. Nearby were two small-scale chintz-covered swivel rockers.

That's one way to keep a guy from planting himself and staying, Amos thought. *Put him in a chair that cramps his style.*

The only other place for a guest to sit was the straight chair next to the table-desk. Obviously she didn't hold meetings here—not large ones, at any rate.

Erika rose from behind the table. Her off-white suit was crisp and fresh, as if she'd just put it on for the occasion. He was surprised she'd gone to that much trouble.

"Thanks for coming, Amos."

Thanks for coming? He tried for a lighter note. "I thought we had a wedding scheduled."

"Oh. Yes. Of course. I hope you don't mind that it's here—in the conference room. Kelly's done a wonderful job decorating it."

"A conference room?"

"Well, it seemed a little hypocritical to be married in a church, under the circumstances." She sounded defensive.

"And a pastor might not be amused by our ninety-day limit, since it would hurt his earned-run average."

"His what?"

"His statistics—successful marriages versus number of divorces." Amos wasn't surprised that she seemed a little absentminded. No doubt she was anxious to get this necessary step over with so she could move on to acquiring Kate La Croix's company.

"And the courthouse would have been hard to secure," she added. "The press, you know—you can't keep them out of a public building."

"I'm just surprised you can fit everyone in a conference room. Even on such short notice, there must be lots of people who'd like to be at your wedding. You know— friends, family."

"Not that many, really. And what about you? You didn't invite anyone at all."

That was true enough, though he'd hoped that she wouldn't notice. "I'm sorry this isn't the wedding of your dreams," he said quietly.

"My dreams?" She sounded as if she didn't understand.

"You know. The cathedral, the white gown with a train, sixteen bridesmaids…"

She shook her head. "All just useless trappings."

"And a husband you're in love with," Amos finished.

"That's a myth, you know. Being in love is no more lasting than orange blossom and music." There was a tap on the door. "Yes, Kelly?"

The assistant put her head in. "The judge is here, and the guests are all waiting."

Erika took a deep breath and held her head high. "Then let's get this over with," she said.

No more lasting than orange blossom and music… Stanford Forrester III, Amos thought grimly, had a lot to answer for.

CHAPTER FIVE

IT SEEMED to Erika that the conference room was filled with fog so dense that it was deafening as well as blinding. Or perhaps it was just her brain which wasn't operating properly, since no one besides her seemed to be having any problem seeing and hearing.

Of all the times to bring up love, she thought irritably. Amos was the last person she would have expected to broach the topic at all, but to do it right then...

Love. It wasn't ever a subject she wanted to think about, and especially not in the short minutes before her wedding. She'd seen the aftermath of love. Or, rather, the aftermath of the myth of love.

Stanford Forrester had been a playboy, and everyone had known it. But the myth said that he would change for the sake of love. Or he would change when he himself fell in love. Or perhaps he would change when he found the love of a good woman...

But he hadn't. Whether he'd ever considered himself in love or not, Erika didn't know, and she didn't particularly care. He must have felt something different toward Erika's mother, for she was the only one of his flames that he'd married. Even after he was free again, there had never been any hint that he was considering another walk down the aisle.

But there wasn't any question in Erika's mind that her mother had considered herself in love with him, or that she had been a good woman who had done her best. Her feelings hadn't been enough to change Stanford Forrester from playboy to loving husband, but she had refused to give up, because love was supposed to change him.

So—having watched her mother suffer—Erika had grown up suspecting that love was nothing more than a romantic myth. And then, just when she had managed to convince herself that perhaps she'd been wrong, that maybe it was possible for love to be more than a fairy tale, Denby Miles had come along....

"Erika," Amos whispered. "We could use an answer here."

"I do," she said automatically. The words seemed to drop into the fog, swallowed up in the silence of the room. That must mean her answer hadn't been the right one, the expected one. "I will," she added hastily. "Yes. I mean—"

"That pretty well covers it," the judge said with a smile. "Do you have rings?"

Amos reached into his pocket.

The judge looked at Erika. She shook her head. It would hardly be smart to admit the truth—that she'd entirely forgotten to ask her fiancé whether he wanted a wedding ring. Though she couldn't imagine that he would, so it was no big deal.

She had to admit to feeling curious about the ring he produced, though. She'd assumed Stephen had chosen a wedding ring as well as the engagement diamond, but she hadn't seen it.

She held out her hand, expecting that he'd just slide the wedding band up next to her diamond. Instead he gently tugged the engagement ring off her finger and put the wedding band in its place. "Closest to the heart," he said, and replaced the diamond.

Romantic nonsense, she wanted to say.

She looked down at her hand, still resting in his. The

platinum wedding band was severely plain, wide, and sleek. Though it wasn't flashy like the diamond, in its own way it was just as attention-getting. Which was pretty much the point, after all.

"By the power invested in me by the State of New York, I pronounce you husband and wife," the judge said, and the guests burst into applause.

Erika had almost forgotten the guests. She hadn't wanted any kind of fuss at all, just the absolute necessities of a judge, two witnesses and a piece of legal documentation. But Kelly had arranged for champagne and hors d'oeuvres and invited the office staff to attend. "Nobody will expect a big blowout," she had said. "But there's a difference between keeping the wedding small and quiet, and hiding out as if you're ashamed of yourself."

So, though there was nothing Erika wanted more than just to go home, she began to circulate through the crowd.

"Of course there was no kiss," she heard Amos say behind her. "But just wait till I don't have to be careful of the makeup."

Kiss. She'd forgotten all about the obligatory kiss. Well, it was too late now.

She moved through the guests, chatting and sipping champagne.

She noticed the director of marketing talking earnestly to the advertising executive in charge of the fall campaign, and smiled.

"What's the joke?" Amos asked, coming up beside her to swap her nearly empty champagne flute for a full one.

"Oh, I was just wondering what the two guys in the corner would say if they knew they missed out on—what did you call it? The husband sweepstakes?"

He glanced at the duo. "You're not serious. They were both on your list?"

"Well, it was only a fleeting thought. What's wrong with them, anyway?"

"One's oily and the other's naive," Amos said. "Who else did you think about?"

She certainly wasn't going to tell him about the delivery boy from the Chinese restaurant. "Why do you want to know?"

"So I can count them all to put myself to sleep at night."

"Sorry. You'll have to settle for sheep." She strolled toward the corner. "Are you two talking about the photo shoot for the fall ad campaign?"

"Business before pleasure," the ad man said. "Though with a few extra days to plan, I was thinking—"

"Extra days?" Erika said. "The shoot's tomorrow."

The marketing director turned pink and muttered something about assuming that she'd want to postpone it.

"What's the matter?" Erika asked. "Of course I don't want to postpone it."

"I believe he's suggesting," Amos said lazily, "that since this is your wedding night, you might not want to get up early and face a bunch of cameras."

The marketing director was beet-red and stammering.

"Oh," said Erika. "Well, as a professional, I certainly will—"

"—Need to start later," Amos inserted smoothly. "If you two will arrange for her to have a couple of extra hours to pull herself together in the morning, I'll promise to get her into bed early tonight."

The ad manager laughed as if it was the best joke he'd ever heard. The marketing director had turned so red that he practically glowed.

"In fact," Amos added, "now that we've greeted everyone, I'm more than ready to go home. How about you, darling? Wouldn't you like to be alone?"

Alone. It sounded so good.

Except, of course, that the definition of *alone* was now a whole lot different than it used to be.

When they reached the door of her apartment, Erika fumbled for her keys, but the miniature compact which served her as a key ring had migrated all the way to the bottom of her bag. By the time she found it, Amos had unlocked the door, pushed it open, and dropped his key into his pocket once more.

She told herself not to be ridiculous. Of course he would need a key of his own. If she had remembered it earlier, she would have asked Stephen to have one made from the master set he kept. So why should it bother her that Amos had gone ahead and done it himself?

"Are you annoyed about the key?" Amos asked. "Or are you just standing here because you're waiting for me to carry you over the threshold in proper honeymoon style?"

"Don't be ridiculous." She stepped past him and into the foyer. "I was just startled, that's all. But of course you needed a key so you could move your things up here today."

At first glance, however, the apartment didn't seem any different than when she had left it that morning. Whatever he had brought with him, it wasn't in evidence. "You did move your belongings, didn't you?" she asked.

"Of course. I just didn't think you'd appreciate tripping over my stuff, so it's all in the guest room and the den, out of your way."

It was very thoughtful of him. And it was completely crazy of her to want him to have been a slob just so she could yell a little and let off steam.

Furthermore, it was absolutely clear to Erika from the

gleam in his eyes that Amos knew exactly what she was thinking.

If he kept that up, Erika thought, the man was going to get mighty annoying.

The gleam in his eyes had gone, she realized, and was replaced by a steely determination. "I think we need to get something straight before we go any further," Amos said.

"What now? If you're going to start making demands within hours of the wedding—"

"The only thing I'm demanding is that you start acting as if you take this whole thing seriously."

"Of course I'm—"

"No, you're not, Erika. You went through the motions, that's all. You were barely paying attention to what the judge was saying. You didn't even notice that we skipped the ceremonial kiss. You told your ad guys that the photo shoot would be business as usual. In short, you might as well have announced that this marriage is going to make no difference in your life."

Well, it isn't, she wanted to say.

"You conveniently forgot to give me a key—what's that if not mixed feelings? And right now you're itching to pick a fight—and you would be even if we were in public. At that rate, how long do you think it'll be before the *Sentinel* starts speculating about why you got married in the first place?"

The truth in his words flicked her like a whip, and Erika struck back. "You're just annoyed that I forgot to ask you about a wedding ring."

"That didn't help the image any," he agreed.

"So do you want one?"

"Of course not."

"Then what's the big deal? Lots of married guys don't wear wedding rings—even the ones who own them."

The silence seemed to stretch out like warm taffy. "Your father?" His voice was gentle. "Or are you talking about your ex-fiancé?"

"Denby could hardly be married on the sly—or had you forgotten that he's engaged again? Not that it's any of your business."

"No, and it's not the subject of this discussion, either. If you want anyone to take this marriage seriously, you're going to have to start acting as if you believe in it. And if you don't—well, then perhaps you should ask yourself why you bothered."

"Thanks for the words of wisdom. If you've quite finished..."

"Oh, yes, I'm finished. At least I'm going to stop wasting my breath." He sat down and picked up the morning newspaper, still lying where Erika had dropped it on the hassock which served as a coffee table.

Well, if he was going to occupy her living room, Erika decided, she'd just go somewhere else. Like downstairs to the gym so she could work off some frustration on the treadmill.

Oh, that would look good on your wedding night, Erika.

She closed the door of her bedroom with a thump and sat down on the edge of the bed.

He's right, you know. He saved you, back there in the conference room.

Much as she'd been annoyed at the time by the suggestive remark about how eager he was to get her into bed, she had to admit that the ploy had worked exactly as he'd intended. By amusing the ad executive and embarrassing the marketing manager, he'd effectively prevented either of them from asking more questions.

The fact was that Amos was carrying out his part of this agreement brilliantly, while she herself was acting half-hearted and doubtful, exactly as he'd accused. She might as well call up the *Sentinel* and invite them to ask questions.

She pushed herself up from the bed and went back to the living room. He was half-hidden behind the newspaper, and he didn't lower it when she came in.

"I'm sorry," she said. "You're right. I'll do better."

He didn't look up. "Good."

He didn't sound as if he believed her. She couldn't blame him; she'd learned herself not to put much faith in promises. Promises were easy. They didn't count, only results did.

Obviously she'd have to prove herself—starting right now. "Are you hungry, Amos? I only had a couple of tidbits from the hors d'oeuvre table. We could get a pizza delivered or something."

"That would be fine."

"Any preference on what kind?"

"I'm easy when it comes to pizza." He put the paper aside. "Just no green olives, please."

She phoned in the order and dug her wallet out of her handbag. What had happened to her brain lately? He could read all kinds of Freudian meanings into the fact that she'd forgotten to arrange to get him a key, but in fact, she'd also forgotten to stop at the bank, and she was too low on cash to pay for the pizza. Was there anything she actually *had* remembered to do?

"Amos, I'm sorry—but I have to go into the den to get my checkbook."

"Sorry? For what?"

"Because I'm intruding. I told you to use the room, but then I forgot to get my stuff out before you moved in."

"Hey, it's still your den. We can share. Tell you what— I promise never to peek at your checkbook, you promise never to look at my first draft, and we'll both be happy."

"Well, that seems fair." Still, she hesitated outside the closed door of the extra room she used as an at-home office. *What do you expect, Erika?* she mocked herself. If he'd tacked up X-rated posters, he'd have made an excuse to go get the checkbook himself rather than let her go in.

She pushed the door open.

She'd left the desktop clear after she'd last paid her bills—now there was a laptop computer sitting squarely in the center. On the floor beside the desk was a corrugated box, the kind that businesses used for long-term storage of records. Research materials for his book, perhaps? Or office supplies?

But there seemed to be nothing else newly added to the room. Amos had told her that he had stashed all his belongings in the guest room and the den. But since there wasn't much in the den, that must mean the guest room was full—or else he hadn't brought much with him.

Not that it was any of her business, really.

She filled out two checks, put the checkbook away and went back to the living room. "And here I thought you were the old-fashioned sort," she said. "Down in the office that day, you were writing your book with a pen on a legal pad."

"Security," he said briefly.

"You mean you didn't want to take a chance on your computer vanishing if you had to step out?"

"Not exactly. But I'm the only one who can read my writing, so leaving a notepad lying around isn't a risk. Not that it would have mattered, no more than I got written that day."

"Well, that will change starting tomorrow." She handed him a check. "Would you mind filling this in for the pizza guy when he comes? I'm going to go change clothes—

maybe have a quick bath. And here." She handed him a second check.

"What's this for?"

"You'll need some spending money. I thought the easiest way would be if I write you a check every week."

"A weekly allowance. How nice." His tone was flat.

"If you'd rather handle it some other way, Amos—"

"This is fine."

"Or if you need more—"

"I said, this is fine."

"I just thought you'd rather not have to ask me for money every time you want to go out for lunch." Erika had never felt so awkward. "Look, you said you wanted me to take this more seriously. I'm trying, all right?"

His jaw tightened. "Yes," he said finally. "Of course you are." The corners of his mouth turned upward, but the smile didn't seem to reach his eyes. "My macho side kicked in a little just then. The whole idea of being a kept man…"

"You're not. Think of me as a patron of the arts in the best Renaissance tradition."

"I'll give it a shot," he said dryly.

"You can dedicate the book to me. And when you hit the bestseller list, you can take me out for drinks to pay me back."

He glanced at the check again. "It would take some pretty special drinks."

"Well, I didn't say where we were going to have them."

This time his smile was real—and Erika felt warm and rewarded as she basked in its glow.

Photo shoots might sound glamorous to someone who had never experienced one, but for Erika, they were a trial from start to finish. The day always started with submitting to a makeup artist who used her as a living canvas, followed by hairstylists and wardrobe people who fussed over her for another era or two. Then there were endless hours of being treated like a rag doll, placed in a pose, and asked to hold it while the photographer shot an instant photo for the art director and the advertising executive to argue about. Then they'd move her arm or turn her head, touch up the makeup, shift one or two of the battery of lights which hung from the ceiling on adjustable brackets, spray a stray hair, shoot another instant photo, and start the waiting and arguing all over again. By the time everybody was convinced they'd got the shots they needed, tempers were always frayed and she was usually so stiff she could barely move.

She supposed that models who did this every day either got used to it or were egotistical enough about their beauty to find all the attention flattering. But even after three years of regular shoots, Erika hadn't gotten used to it, and she didn't find it any fun to be surrounded by sycophants, either. Still, it was only a few days a year—and the personal price was well worth it when she considered the benefit to the company.

However, getting a late start had simply put everyone into a bad mood, and by the time they took the first break they'd managed to shoot only a single roll of film. Erika took the icy water bottle that Kelly handed her and considered rubbing it across her forehead, hot from the intense lights that had been focused on her all morning. But then they'd have to start over with the makeup artist, and things would be even more delayed. So she settled for a long drink instead—using a straw so she'd do the minimal damage to her lipstick.

On the other side of the bank of lights, the room seemed dark, shadowy, and full of indistinct shapes—there were an incredible number of crew and support staff. Erika's eyes were still accustomed to the bright lights she'd been facing, so she had to grope her way around the camera tripod and between even more lights—these clamped to wheeled stands—in order to get to a reasonably comfortable couch in one corner. She sank down with a sigh, disregarding for the moment the carefully pressed royal-blue satin blouse she was wearing. She loosened one pearl earring—it had been fastened so tightly that her earlobe ached—and put her head back against a pillow that someone had propped there.

Probably someone sneaking a nap between tasks, she thought. Now that was an inviting thought...

A shadow moved closer, and Amos perched on the arm of the couch. "You hate it, don't you?"

She sat up straight. "What in heaven's name are you doing here? And how long have you been watching?"

"An hour or so. I came to keep an eye on my adored bride to make sure they don't overtire you."

"In other words, you're just poking your nose in to see what's going on."

"That, too." The description didn't seem to concern him.

But then it wouldn't, Erika thought, because it was all part of the act. He wanted the crew to see him as the brand-new, overprotective husband who couldn't bear to be separated from his wife.

"No one seemed surprised when I turned up," he added.

"Or maybe they're just good at concealing it."

"Unless they're used to you having visitors?"

"No—I prefer a private session."

"That's pretty hilarious—since I've counted thirty-two people already and I'm fairly sure I haven't seen them all yet."

The entire crew seemed to have vanished at once, however. Though they weren't absolutely alone, there were only a few technicians in the room. One was readjusting the bank of spotlights mounted on ceiling brackets right next to the camera, another—acting as a stand-in model— was lounging on the taped mark where Erika had been posing, and a couple more were moving props around the studio. For once, no one was paying any attention to Erika.

Except of course for Amos, who was watching her intently. "You hate it, don't you?" he repeated.

She thought about denying it, but she was just too tired. "I didn't know it showed."

"Maybe not to all of them." His gesture took in the whole room. "But then I'm not one of the trees, so I can see the forest more clearly. Why do you do it, if you hate it?"

"It's only four times a year."

"Let someone else do it."

"Maybe someday." She swallowed another gulp of water and stood up. "Let's get back to work, everybody, and get this done."

Amos didn't move. "I see. You don't like doing it, but you won't give up control."

"That's not true. I don't—" Why was she arguing with him? What difference did it make what he thought? Annoyed at herself, Erika swung around on her heel to walk back to her mark, and slammed into one of the newly adjusted lights right next to the camera.

The shock wave of the blow was so intense that she didn't know for sure where the impact point was—her temple? Her eyebrow? Her cheekbone? They all seemed to hurt with equal intensity.

The impact knocked her off balance. Trying to regain her footing, she caught her toe on one of the wheeled light stands and went down hard. Even the rubbery surface of the commercial carpet couldn't completely cushion the shock of her hip hitting the floor.

The room was revolving. She groaned and lay still.

When she opened her eyes, Amos was crouching over her. "Don't try to move," he ordered. "You hit pretty hard."

"Funny." She clenched her teeth against the waves of pain. "I'd noticed that myself."

The technician who had been adjusting the lights was looking over Amos's shoulder. "Wow," he said, with a note of admiration in his voice. "That's gonna be a heck of a shiner."

Instinctively Erika put a hand up to her face to check the damage. Amos grabbed her wrist and kept her from touching it.

"Am I bleeding?"

He shook his head. "There's no cut. It's a good thing you hit the light squarely instead of on the point."

"The whole side of my face feels like I've been hit with a brick, and I'm supposed to be grateful?"

"Yes. It could have damaged your eye." He looked up at the technician. "Do you suppose you could make yourself useful and turn one of those spotlights this direction, instead of just standing there staring? And send somebody for ice." He picked up the water bottle Erika had dropped when she fell and held it to the side of her face. She winced away from the cold plastic, but even trying to move hurt, so she lay still.

More faces appeared around his, bending over her. There were shrieks, exclamations, shouted questions, discussion of an ambulance and a doctor.

"Would everybody just shut up," Amos said. "If she doesn't already have a headache, you're giving her one."

"I've got one," Erika muttered.

A nervous assistant arrived with a double handful of ice cubes, water already dripping from between her fingers. Amos looked around, grabbed a towel off the makeup artist's table, gathered up the ice cubes and laid the pack carefully against Erika's eye.

"That's a hundred-dollar matte towel," the artist shrieked.

"Good. Now it's a priceless part of a first-aid kit." Amos leaned closer to Erika. "Now that the shock's wearing off, do you think you can get up? Or do we need to get an ambulance?"

"My hip hurts, too." She stretched out her foot and rotated her ankle. "But it's okay, I just bumped it when I fell. Yes, I can get up."

"Then let's go get this checked out."

"But the photo shoot—"

"You're finished for the day," Amos said flatly.

Erika put a fingertip carefully to her cheek, under the ice bag. The flesh felt puffy. The normally bony ridge at the corner of her eye didn't feel bony anymore.

"But if you insist on continuing," Amos went on cheerfully, "I'm sure the next shots would be worth big bucks—at least to the *Sentinel.*"

Erika refused to go to the hospital, and Amos had to admit that he saw her point. A photo of Erika Forrester sitting in a crowded emergency room holding a bag of ice to her face would definitely be worth a thousand words—and probably more than a thousand dollars. And since she swore she hadn't been knocked unconscious even for an instant, and there was no cut and no blood, he gave in and took her home instead.

Stephen called a kindly retired doctor who lived on the third floor, and he came upstairs to look Erika over. "Keep a close watch on her for a few hours," he told Amos, and showed him how to check that the pupils of her eyes were reacting normally. "But if she isn't having any trouble by this evening, I think she's going to get off easy."

Amos saw him out and came back to Erika's bedroom. She had flung a hand up over her face—he wasn't sure whether she was protecting her eyes or trying to hide the damage. Right now, it was hard to tell whether the side of her face was red because of the blow itself or the ice pack. But there was no doubt about the swelling. By morning it was going to be, as the lighting technician had said, one heck of a shiner.

"Get off easy," she muttered. "Not having any trouble. Maybe I should switch heads with him and see how he likes having his skull throbbing."

"Nah. You wouldn't look good wearing his crew cut."

She tried to smile. "It was nice of him to make a house call, anyway. If my head would just stop hurting—"

Amos handed her a glass of water and a couple of pain-killers. "Need some fresh ice?"

"Why? Has mine gone stale?" She shifted restlessly. "Sorry. I feel so stupid for doing this to myself. And I'm sure this isn't your idea of fun, either."

"For better or for worse," he said lightly. He turned the lights down. "Try to rest, Erika. I'll be out in the living room if you need anything."

"I'd rather—" She stopped suddenly. "No, that's just silly."

"What do you want?"

For a minute he thought she wasn't going to answer. "I was wondering if you'd stay with me. But I'm sure you have other things you'd rather do."

The quaver in her voice was so faint he almost didn't

hear it. He wondered if she knew it was there. Probably not, he thought, or she wouldn't have said anything at all.

He sat down on the edge of the bed and reached for her hand. Her fingers fluttered for a moment and then went lax in his grip as she drifted off to sleep.

He sat there for a long time, listening to the soft rhythm of her breathing.

For better or for worse... He had said it almost without thinking. But what in the hell had he gotten himself into?

CHAPTER SIX

ERIKA woke up slowly, afraid to move but not immediately clear about why she felt that way. Then memory returned and she lay still, taking stock. Her head was no longer throbbing, though there was still a dull ache around her right eye. The ice pack had slipped off the side of her face, or else she'd turned away from the cold while she slept, but a careful touch told her that the skin was still puffy and very tender. Her hip didn't hurt anymore, so that pain must have been more a matter of the jolt of her fall than of actual injury.

She vaguely remembered Amos coming in to check on her several times. Had she really asked him to stay with her? What a baby he must think her, to want company in the middle of the day, just because the room was dark!

She swung her feet off the bed and sat up.

Almost instantly the half-closed door of her bedroom swung wide. Amos paused in the doorway. "Feeling better?"

"All things considered, yes." She stood up a little too quickly and caught at the tall post of the bed for balance. "You must have been sitting right outside the door."

"Just keeping an eye on you."

She waved a hand at the side of her face. "How does it look by now?"

"Not good. But nothing to commit suicide over."

Well, she'd asked for that. She'd been hoping for reassurance, of course, but she should have known better than to ask Amos for his opinion unless she wanted a direct answer. She ought to have learned that much about him from their first encounter.

Still, she was irritated at his reaction—did he honestly think she was so vain as to kill herself over a black eye?

"Come on, Amos," she said irritably. "I've learned a few tricks with makeup over the years. I can cover up darn near any—" She glanced at her reflection in the big mirror above her dressing table and stifled a shriek.

She'd realized from the single tentative touch when she first woke that her cheek was still swollen. But now she saw that the whole side of her face had puffed up, and the area directly around her eye was already purplish-black. The bruise extended from above her eyebrow to well below her cheekbone, from the corner of her nose almost to her ear.

"You were saying?" Amos asked politely.

Erika didn't bother to answer. She sat down at the dressing table and flipped a switch to turn on the lights surrounding the mirror. The low-powered but shadowless bulbs made the bruise look even worse. Funny—she wouldn't have thought it was possible to make it stand out even more. "I'm going to start experimenting."

"You might as well try it. At least it'll give you something to do."

"Thanks for your confidence." Erika dampened a sponge with cleansing cream and began removing the remaining photo makeup. Much of it had already disappeared, rubbed off by the ice packs and towels, but until she got rid of the rest, she couldn't truly judge what she was working with. She suspected, however, that this was going to be the biggest cosmetic challenge she'd ever faced. It would take a tank-car load of foundation to cover this up.

"Maybe a wide-brimmed hat with a black veil," he offered. "I'll bet Stephen could find—"

"I might as well take out an ad as to show up wearing anything of the sort." She wiped gently and winced.

"Careful—pressing too hard might make it worse."

"Worse than it already is? That would be flat impossible. Would you mind bringing me an orange juice? There are bottles in the refrigerator."

"You don't want an audience while you work. All right, I can take a hint."

Finally she was rid of the last traces of the thick stagy paint, and the contrast of the bruised area to her normally fair skin made the damage even more apparent.

Amos hadn't come back yet when she heard the chime of the doorbell. She leaped to her feet. What if a photographer had eluded Stephen in the lobby? "Amos, don't answer that!"

"It'll be Kelly," he called back. "She phoned earlier to say she'd be over."

Erika settled back on the bench and stared at her face. A picture hat with a veil? Not good enough. It would take a blanket over her head to completely conceal this.

But why should she act as if she were ashamed of what had happened? She'd do the best she could to hide the damage, of course, but it wasn't as if there had been anything fishy going on. She'd had an accident, that was all.

She reached for a creamy foundation a shade darker than the one she usually used and began to methodically stroke it over her face, slowing as she reached the puffy areas. The tenderness of the skin was a problem she hadn't considered before. If she couldn't even feather the edges…

She could hear the murmur of voices from the hallway, but the lighter, feminine one didn't sound at all like Kelly.

Puzzled, she finally peeked around the corner and down the hall to see what was going on.

The front door was half-open and Amos was blocking it, with one hand on the door and the other on the jamb. Just beyond his shoulder, Erika could see a frizz of red hair—the top of a woman's head. She remembered the hair, but she had a moment's trouble picturing the face that went with it. It belonged to one of the neighbors, she was certain of that much.

"I completely understand that you're not the manager anymore." The woman was talking very fast. "And I know you're busy writing. I'm so impressed to know a real author! But Stephen's all tied up this afternoon, and I wondered if you could take a teeny little minute and give me a hand."

"What's Stephen tied up with?" Amos asked.

Good move, Erika thought. He hadn't actually said no, though it was quite clear to Erika what he'd meant. *Now just edge her out, Amos...*

"The lobby seemed to be full of strangers when I came in," the woman said earnestly. "I don't know why they're all here, though. Do you?"

Erika didn't realize how far she'd leaned into the hallway as she'd listened, and she was unaware of making any sound. But suddenly the neighbor's head jerked to one side so she could see past Amos's shoulder and down the hall. Erika found herself staring straight into the woman's wide brown eyes.

The woman gave a little screech, and Erika pulled back into her bedroom. Thank heaven, she thought, that she'd been standing in the shadow of the door.

"I didn't know *she* was home," the neighbor said accusingly.

I don't doubt that for an instant, Erika thought. *Or you wouldn't have come over at all.*

From behind her bedroom door, however, all she could hear was the rise and fall of voices, not the actual words. Before long, the front door closed with a soft snap, and she heard a single set of footsteps coming down the hall.

"It's safe now. Sorry about the delay." Amos gave her an appraising look as he handed her a bottle of orange juice and uncapped his own. "It doesn't look as if you're making much progress."

"Thanks—you make me feel so much better." Erika picked up a brush again and studied her reflection. Unfortunately he was dead-right. She hadn't improved the situation at all. She reached for the sponge again and began to wipe off the makeup she'd so carefully applied.

"Giving up?"

"No, I'm just starting over."

"Well, I'm not a medical man. But I'd think it would be better to leave it uncovered anyway rather than take a chance on slowing the healing process."

"If I can cover it up well enough, what difference does it make if it takes a day or two longer to heal?" Erika twisted the plastic top off the orange juice bottle and took a long drink. "You're quite the popular guy around here. If you thought they'd give up because you were playing hard-to-get, you've obviously underestimated what a challenge you are."

His eyes held an odd gleam. "And the sort of woman I'm dealing with?"

"Well, that, too. *'I'm so impressed to know a real author!'*" she mimicked. "Honestly—some women are just dense. Or they think that men are."

Amos paused with his bottle halfway to his mouth.

"Meaning what?" he asked politely. "That I'm not at all impressive?"

"No. I meant that if she really respected your work, she wouldn't be interrupting it to ask you to—what was it she wanted, anyway?"

"Sorry. If I'd realized you would want a complete report, I'd have made sure to ask."

Erika looked at him in astonishment. "What's the matter with you? If you want to help her out, I'm not going to stand in your way."

"I wasn't planning to rush over to her rescue, no."

"Well, that sounds more like the Amos I know. Oh. I think I see now. If you mean I'm interrupting your work just as she did—well, getting hurt wasn't my idea." She didn't look at him. "Besides, I'm not the one who came to a photo shoot uninvited. You could have been working this morning, but instead, you were hassling me, and that's why I ran into the light in the first place."

He said calmly, "I wondered how long it would be before I got the blame."

Erika bit her lip. "That's not what I meant, exactly. I'm not saying it was your fault."

"Just that if I hadn't been there, it wouldn't have happened. Right?"

The bell rang again, and he got up to answer it.

"Amos, be careful," she called after him. "You heard the neighbor say the lobby was full of people. If there are reporters and photographers down there, one of them could slip past Stephen."

"I thought you believed Stephen was invincible," he said over his shoulder.

This time, however, he returned in just moments with Kelly following close behind. He didn't come in, but Kelly stepped inside the bedroom, took one look at Erika and gasped.

"What is the matter with you?" Erika snapped. "I know it's not pretty, but I'm not exactly the Beast from the fairy tale, either. For heaven's sake, Kelly—"

"But it's gotten so much worse! What are you going to do?"

Erika took another look in the mirror. Without any makeup at all, the bruise did look worse. It seemed to be even angrier than it had been just a few minutes ago, before she'd started smoothing makeup onto the abused skin. Maybe Amos had a point about leaving it alone.

It was time to face facts. No matter how hard she tried, the best she'd be able to do was knock down the contrast, not eliminate it altogether. There would be no hiding this.

She surrendered and stood up. "There's nothing much I can do," she admitted. "Let's go into the living room where we can be comfortable."

Kelly nodded slowly. "And we can talk about how to handle everything. I brought your calendar, so we can decide what to postpone, what you can handle by conference call—"

"What are you talking about?" Erika led the way into the living room and stopped on the threshold.

Amos's laptop computer was on the coffee table, humming, and he was sitting on the couch, staring at the screen.

"Sorry," she said hastily. "I didn't mean to intrude. I didn't realize you were working in here."

"Come on in. I only moved to keep a closer eye on you." He shut the computer and leaned back on the couch, dangling his orange juice bottle between two fingers. "Want something to drink, Kelly?"

"Sure," she said, but she was still staring at Erika. "You can't go out in public looking this way."

"Of course I'm going out," Erika said flatly. "I have a business to run. I can't just disappear till this is gone."

"You have to. You cannot be seen like this."

"It was an accident, Kelly."

"Accident or not," Kelly said firmly, "it's a public relations nightmare. The Face of Ladylove cannot be seen with a black eye."

"It's not like the fall ad campaign is going to use it as a theme."

"But that's just it, Erika. Wherever you go, you're a walking ad for the company. So what does it say about Ladylove when your makeup can't camouflage a bruise?"

Erika opened her mouth to argue, and closed it again. "This is not your average bruise," she said finally.

"Well, we market Ladylove products as not your average cosmetics, too. Look," Kelly said, "I came over here to warn you about the powwow that the marketing people and the advertising people and the public relations people had, starting about three minutes after you left the building. I thought they were overreacting, but now—"

Erika was starting to get a really bad feeling. "Warn me? What are they up to now?"

"They were plotting damage control. I thought they were being ridiculous to worry about it, but now that I've seen you—" She sighed. "Erika, they're right. You can't go out in public like this."

"You're seeing me at the absolute worst."

Amos came back with an orange juice for Kelly. "I hate to disagree," he said, "but I think it'll be even blacker by morning."

"Oh, that's comforting," Erika snapped.

"Two or three days and it'll be turning purple. Another three and it'll be green, and then it'll fade to yellow—"

"Thank you very much," Erika said. "Actually you've

pretty much proved my point, Amos. I can't be out of commission for a week while this goes away.''

Amos shrugged. ''What are the options?''

Erika mentally ticked off the things she'd already considered and rejected. Picture hat, blanket…The only new
one she could think of was wearing a paper bag over her
head—and the problem with that was having to cut out
holes for her eyes, which meant she'd be right back where
she started. A paper bag combined with very large sun-
glasses, perhaps…

''What about the makeup they were using today for the
photo shoot?'' Amos asked. ''That stuff looked like it was
industrial strength.''

''It is,'' Erika said. ''And it photographs beautifully—
but in person anyone wearing it looks like a corpse. You
only saw me in dim light today, and then later I was wearing a towel and an ice pack—so you didn't get the full
effect.''

''Come to think of it,'' he mused, ''you *did* look pretty
well dead on your feet. You mean you seriously don't use
the real stuff in the ads? If the famous Face of Ladylove
isn't really wearing Ladylove products at all, that's false
advertising.''

''Of course it's really our product. It's a special line
we've formulated especially for actresses and models, just
for photographs.''

''And even that wouldn't be strong enough,'' Kelly said.
''Not to cover this…difficulty.''

''That's why I think the only sensible thing to do is face
it,'' Erika argued. ''I'll just admit I smacked into a light,
and I'll go on with my life. A couple of days of speculation
and there won't be anything left to say.''

''Don't bet on it,'' Kelly warned. ''I tried to talk the

marketing and PR and ad people into waiting a while before they did anything, to see how bad it actually was, but—"

"I don't think I'm going to like this," Erika muttered.

"They felt if it turned out not to be too bad, then it wouldn't matter much what anybody said. But if it was awful, then they needed to do something immediately, to kill the story before it could get a good start."

Erika put her face in her hands—and hastily lifted it out again, because the pressure of her fingertips hurt.

"So they assembled everybody who was at the shoot and threatened them with immediate termination if they talked. The official policy is that nothing happened to you today. We got the shot we needed in a hurry, and you went home to enjoy your honeymoon."

Erika gritted her teeth. "I'll fire every last one of them."

"They were only doing what they thought was best," Kelly argued. "You know there are always reporters nosing around everything you do. And you have to admit, Erika, you were hardly in any position to be making decisions right then."

Amos leaned back into the depths of the couch. "So if they've already denied that anything happened…"

"And then you show up with a black eye and a story about running into a light…" Kelly added.

Nobody would believe it, that was sure. They would add two plus two and end up with a whole lot more. The *Sentinel*'s sum would probably be somewhere around ninety-seven.

Erika was stuck.

"I hope you have some hobbies, honey," Amos said. "Because it appears you're going to have some time on your hands to enjoy them."

They spread Erika's calendar out on the kitchen table, and it took more than an hour for her and Kelly to hash out the fine points—to decide what could be passed along to someone else to take care of, what Erika could handle by phone, and what could be put off until she was back in the office in a week. "A week," she muttered, hardly believing what she was saying.

"You'd better figure on ten days," Amos said as he came in with the bundle of mail which had just been delivered. "Just in case."

Erika tried to ignore him. *It can't possibly be more than a week,* she told herself. *I'm a fast healer.*

After Kelly left with a list of cryptic-looking instructions, Erika went looking for Amos. It didn't take long to find him—and that, she figured, was going to be part of the problem.

He'd apparently taken his computer back into the den, for it wasn't on the coffee table any more. But he was still settled in the living room. When she came in, he was lounging on the couch, a notepad open on his knee and a pen in hand.

She wondered whether he was contemplating his story or his life.

She had to admit to feeling a little sympathy for him. This was hardly the way he'd expected things to work out, either. He'd come to the photo shoot in an attempt to make the whole scenario look real. It had been a misguided move, perhaps, but she didn't doubt that it had been a sincere one. And now everything was turned upside down.

She cleared her throat.

Amos tore a sheet from the notebook, wadded the paper into a ball and lofted it toward the wastebasket with a professional-looking flick of the wrist. "What can I do for you?"

"We'll need to come to some kind of arrangement. It

wasn't anywhere in my plans to spend all my time at home, and I'm sorry if that's going to throw a wrench into your work. But I can hardly camp out in my bedroom.''

Amos shrugged. "It's your apartment. I'm just the houseguest.''

Guest... An idea fluttered through her mind and she seized it. "That's brilliant, Amos.''

He looked a little wary.

"Just because I'm confined to the apartment doesn't mean you can't go anywhere," Erika said eagerly. "You could check into a hotel or go to a resort—'' She stopped, because there was something in his gaze which was almost pitying.

"Without you?'' he said quietly. "But my dear—I couldn't leave my bride alone on our honeymoon. Just think what the *Sentinel* would make of that.''

She bit her lip. He was right, of course—she hadn't even considered how it would look if he moved out just a day or two after the wedding. But the net effect of her accident was that now they were sentenced to each other's company twenty-four hours a day.

How had she ever managed to convince herself that creating a marriage on paper would have no real effect on her life? It had all looked so easy. So sensible. So smooth. So quickly finished. But now...

A week in her apartment under any conditions, and she'd be suffering a massive case of cabin fever. A week of being locked up with a roommate—any roommate—and she'd be climbing the walls. But a week shut up in the same few rooms with Amos, and she would be *hoping* to lose her mind altogether.

The thought of the week possibly stretching to ten days made her feel physically ill.

She'd never before thought of her apartment as a

cramped, tiny space. But by the time this was over, Erika thought grimly, she'd probably be convinced she was living in a closet.

In the confines of the apartment, there was clearly no way to avoid each other, and—feeling a bit perverse—Erika decided not to try to stay out of Amos's way.

As Amos himself had said, it was her apartment, not his. And he was the reason she was injured. Not that she was trying to shift the responsibility for her own carelessness onto him, exactly, but still he'd been the proximate cause. If having her around all the time bothered him, then he had only himself to blame.

As far as Erika was concerned, she wasn't going to waste time holding a grudge about the accident. She would simply ignore him and go on about her life as best she could.

She would start, she decided, by taking advantage of the rare opportunity to do nothing.

She hadn't even had enough energy or time to notice that she was still wearing the royal-blue satin blouse that had been part of the costume for the photo shoot, much less to realize how crumpled and makeup-stained it was from the long day. But finally, with Kelly gone and evening drawing in, she took a long bubble bath and got into the most comfortable nightgown she owned, a silky dark-red floor-length model trimmed in black lace, with a matching brocade robe. Then she took a tray of snacks into the living room.

The room was quiet. The CD which had been playing earlier had finished, and only the muted sounds of traffic from the street far below broke the silence.

Amos was lying on the couch. At first glance, Erika thought he was asleep, but he must have heard the whisper of brocade against the marble floor in the hallway, for he opened one eye when she came in.

"I hope you don't mind," she said. "But this is the only television set in the apartment, and I'd like to watch it tonight."

"Not at all," he said, and sat up.

Erika curled up on the end of the couch, where the leather was still warm from his feet, picked up a carrot stick to munch, and began flipping channels.

"Carrot sticks," he said. "Celery stalks. Green pepper strips."

"Help yourself." It didn't take long to decide that she hadn't missed much by not watching TV on a regular basis. "Have you seen this movie?"

Amos glanced at the screen. "Everybody's seen this movie, Erika. It's older than the two of us put together." He got up and left the room.

One point to me, Erika thought. But she didn't feel quite the sense of triumph she'd expected to, by retaking her living room. She settled deeper into the couch and tried to pick up the thread of the story.

He was back in a few minutes, with an enormous china bowl that she'd never seen before, piled high with popcorn. "Help yourself," he said. "You look surprised. If it's the fact that I can make popcorn, perhaps I should warn you that I can reheat a taco with the best of them, too."

"No, I was just startled that you own a bowl the size of a small swimming pool and obviously intended just for popcorn, since that's what it says on the side. It didn't seem like the sort of thing a single man would carry around."

"Popcorn, tacos, pizza and beer," Amos said, ticking them off on his fingers. "The single man's four main food groups." He set the popcorn bowl squarely in the middle of the couch and lounged at the opposite end.

Since she'd missed the first half hour of the movie, Erika found it hard to get absorbed in the story. And she suspected, though he appeared to be paying attention to the show, that Amos felt just about the same. She could feel him watching her instead of the movie.

Though perhaps that was only her imagination, she tried to tell herself, because she couldn't quite catch him doing it. Whenever she glanced at him from the corner of her eye, he was always looking at the screen.

How perfectly egotistical it was, she told herself, to suspect that just because she was in the room he must be so aware of her that he was sneaking sideways looks. And even if he was watching her, it didn't mean the interest was personal. Maybe, she told herself irritably, he was just studying the purplish blotch on the side of her face as if it was a Rorschach test.

In fact, that was far more likely, since he hadn't shown any particular interest otherwise. He'd kissed her at the literacy banquet for practice and for show, but not because of desire. Those kisses had been purely clinical. And though it was she who had forgotten all about the customary kiss at the end of the wedding ceremony, he'd had such a quick excuse that she couldn't believe he hadn't thought it out ahead of time.

And that was exactly the way she wanted it, Erika told herself. It was just as well that he didn't find her particularly attractive. It was inconvenient enough to have to share a small space with him for days on end, but it would be unbearable if he was putting pressure on her. What would she do, she wondered idly, if—instead of just sitting there watching the movie with the popcorn bowl safely forming a barricade between them—he was leaning closer, putting an arm around her, stroking her throat, inviting her to make love with him... She closed her eyes. She could almost feel his touch, his warmth...

A husky whisper tugged at her senses. "Erika, time for bed. Let's go, sweetheart."

She smiled, amused by how realistic her fantasy sounded, and then as she opened her eyes she realized this wasn't an illusion at all. Her head was against his shoulder, his arm was around her, and his breath was warm against her cheek. She sat up straight, almost banging her face against his in her panic. "What do you think you're doing?"

"Getting you aroused, of course," Amos said.

Her mouth went dry. She couldn't decide which irritated her more—what he was doing, or the blatant way he'd admitted it.

"But only enough to get you across the hall and put you to bed," he added calmly. "Alone. If you were hoping for something more intimate than that, you'll have to wake up completely, because ravishing a semiconscious woman has never been my idea of a good time."

Now Erika was awake, all right—and furious. "That's the only way you'd ever get me into bed!"

"Really? In that case, perhaps you should explain how you define semiconscious."

He sounded as if he really wanted to know, and that made Erika even more irritable. She jumped up. The belt of her brocade robe caught on the arm of the couch. She pulled it loose and stalked across the hall.

"Hey, don't go away angry," Amos advised. "You might be able to change my mind if you work at it. Maybe I've just never met the right semiconscious woman."

Erika hoped he'd follow her, so she'd have the sheer pleasure of slamming her bedroom door in his face.

She was halfway to her room when the doorbell rang.

She almost didn't believe what she was hearing. "Who on earth would be visiting at this hour of the night?"

Amos frowned. "It's not all that late."

Erika ducked into her bedroom.

Amos looked through the peephole and then unlocked the door. "Just a delivery man," he called.

Delivery man? But at this time of day, who would be delivering? And what was he bringing?

Puzzled, Erika peeked around the door frame. She couldn't see the visitor, only a large luggage cart piled high with boxes. "Did you order anything, Amos?" she asked suspiciously. "Or is all this your stuff? I thought you said you'd moved everything yesterday."

"I did," Amos said.

Stephen poked his head around the end of the cart. "They're wedding gifts," he said. "They've been building up downstairs, and this is the first chance I've had to deliver them. I didn't think you'd mind what time it was, since you—" His gaze fell on Erika, and his eyes widened.

"Yes, it's a terrible black eye," she said impatiently, and then realized he wasn't looking at her face at all. He was staring at her red brocade robe. She'd forgotten that her belt had come loose, and she hadn't noticed that as she flounced across the hall, the shawl collar had slipped until it was almost off her shoulders, displaying the lacy straps and bodice of the gown underneath.

Stephen's gaze slid from her to Amos, and for the first time Erika realized that his hair was so disheveled it looked as if she'd been running her fingers through it.

"Since you're not doing anything anyway," Stephen went on, as if he hadn't heard a word she'd said. "I'm not interrupting anything—" He gulped. "Am I?"

CHAPTER SEVEN

ERIKA tugged her robe higher and tightened the belt. "Of course we weren't doing anything, Stephen."

"At least not anything that we want to talk about," Amos agreed cheerfully. "Where do you want to put the plunder, Erika?"

Send it all back, she almost said.

Amos seemed to see the words trembling on her lips and added hastily, "The dining room, I think, since we aren't planning to have dinner parties for a while. And it'll be a convenient place for Erika to write thank-you notes, too. I'll help unload the cart."

He sounded quite pleased with himself, Erika thought. She bit her tongue and waited while the two men maneuvered the cart around the corner into the small dining room.

When everything had been unloaded onto the table and Stephen had manhandled the cart back out to the service elevator, she turned to Amos. "A convenient place for *me* to write thank-you notes?"

"I thought that was a nice, realistic touch. And it has the advantage of being true, too. Since I'll be working in the den—"

"Of course it's also a little chauvinistic, assigning that job to me."

"I see where it could sound that way," Amos conceded. "But it's dead sure that these packages are all from people I don't know—my friends wouldn't even know where to send gifts."

"To say nothing of the fact that you didn't invite anyone

113

to the wedding, so they'd see no reason to give you anything."

"That, too. At any rate, I can hardly be counted on to strike the right chord in a note of thanks to people I don't know. I'm just suggesting a fair division of labor—I'll write the notes to my friends, you write the ones to yours. Now that we have that settled—"

"You just had to be macho, didn't you?"

"What are you talking about?" He sounded honestly surprised. "I wasn't trying to show off my muscles."

"No. I meant the way you suggested that we were…that Stephen had…"

"Oh, I see. What's really bothering you is that you don't like me leaving the impression he was interrupting an intimate episode."

"You don't have to playact for Stephen, for heaven's sake."

"I didn't. I just took advantage of an opportunity when it presented itself. It was very clever of you to shrug halfway out of your robe like that, by the way. You presented an extremely suggestive and effective picture."

She pulled the robe's collar higher. "You know perfectly well I didn't do that on purpose. What was the point of your little performance, anyway? Stephen's already in on the secret. You were just confusing things for no good reason."

"He was in on the secret. But now he doesn't quite know what's going on."

"That's what I mean. There was no point in… Unless you're saying you don't even trust *Stephen?*"

"It's not a matter of trust," Amos said thoughtfully. "But you see, Stephen's just a little too straightforward to be a good liar. He'll be much more convincing now when he issues a denial, because he won't be lying."

Erika shook her head a little, trying to clear it. "You're deliberately trying to mix him up about what's going on?"

"People who know you very well know how you feel about Stephen. So they'll expect that he'll have the whole story, and they'll ask him. Like it or not, as long as we're locked up together in this apartment, Stephen's going to be fielding questions. I'm just making it easier for him to say he doesn't know."

He'd hit the target there, no doubt about it. The fewer people who were in possession of the entire truth, the less chance there was that someone would slip up. In fact, Erika herself had followed the same logic when she hadn't told Kelly every last detail.

Still, having to admit that he was right annoyed her heartily. "Well, in that case, why stop with merely being suggestive?" she said. "Next time he brings up a load of gifts, let's just open the door for him and then throw ourselves down on the floor right in front of the cart and demonstrate. Then he not only wouldn't have to lie, he wouldn't even have to use his imagination!"

Amos didn't say anything, but his long slow smile gave Erika plenty of time to regret that she'd opened her mouth without pausing to think first. "I mean..." she began.

"Oh, don't ruin it just when you're finally getting into the spirit of things." Amos tapped a toe against the marble floor of the entrance foyer. "But I tell you what—let's plan to move into the living room before we start that demonstration. The carpet would be much more comfortable than the cold rock out here."

Since she wasn't going to the office, there was no hurry about getting up at all. At least that was what Erika told herself the next morning. Her hesitation to get dressed and leave her bedroom had nothing to do with Amos and that crackpot conversation last night, she assured herself. They'd both been tired and punchy, that was all. It would probably take a day or two to adjust to the situation, but once they'd gotten the hang of staying out of each other's way, everything would be fine.

She luxuriated in a hot shower and looked at six different outfits. It was tempting to simply put on a fresh nightgown instead of getting dressed at all. But it would hardly be smart. She'd gotten herself in enough hot water last night with the red silk and brocade set, and she wasn't about to ask for more trouble. Even the most innocuous and voluminous white cotton gown was still a nightie—and heaven forbid that Amos get the idea she was issuing some sort of invitation.

But everything else in her closet seemed too formal to wear around the apartment. Her entire wardrobe consisted of suits for work and fancy dresses for evening occasions. Even the few pantsuits she owned were the dressy sort intended for the office, tailored, color-coordinated and far too elegant for a day of lounging around at home—and heaven forbid that Amos get the idea she was dressing up for his sake.

Maybe she should just put on her workout clothes. That would certainly get the message across that she wasn't trying to impress him with her elegance. Of course, most of her exercise things were skintight and elastic so they wouldn't be a hazard on the gym equipment downstairs. And heaven forbid Amos think she was sending an entirely different sort of message...

You can't win, Erika. Just put something on.

She finally chose a pair of navy blue trousers from one pants set and a lighter blue turtleneck from another, ignored her makeup kit and padded down the hall barefoot. With any luck, Amos would already be hard at work in the den and he wouldn't even hear her soft footsteps.

But he wasn't in the den. He was in the kitchen—and someone was with him.

She hovered in the hallway, listening not to the conversation but to the voices. Amos's visitor was a woman—and a woman who was having a good time. That was obvious from the occasional bubble of laughter.

But the woman's voice suddenly sobered. "Maybe you should check on her again, Amos."

Erika relaxed and stepped across the threshold. "Good morning, Kelly. I thought we'd decided to only talk on the phone for a few days because it would draw too much attention if you were coming in and out of the apartment all the time."

"See?" Amos said. "I told you she was fine."

Erika raised an eyebrow at him. "What's this about checking on me?"

"I came down to tell you Kelly was here, but I heard the shower running so I left you alone." He set a plate in front of Kelly, but he was looking at Erika. "Nice job of accessorizing the eye—dressing all in blue that way makes you match from head to toe. Bacon and eggs?"

She shuddered. "No, thanks—but tell me, which of the single man's four food groups does that combination fit into?"

"Roll it into a tortilla shell and it counts as a taco. How about coffee?" He didn't wait for an answer but handed her a steaming cup.

"Real coffee?" Erika inhaled. "This smells almost as good as Kelly's cappuccino."

"It's better," Kelly said. She picked up her fork. "I brought the final draft of the contract on the La Croix deal. Once you sign off on that, the offer can go to Felix."

And once Felix signs and the paperwork all goes through, then all of this will be over, Erika thought. *The sooner we get started, the better.* "I'll read it right now while you have breakfast."

"I also brought over the results from the photo shoot for you to look at."

"That's fast service." Even if it did seem at least a year ago since the last flash had gone off in her face, it was still less than twenty-four hours since the shoot had come to its abrupt end.

"The ad manager was anxious to see what we got," Kelly said.

"He must have been, to have pushed the photo lab like that. How bad are the pictures?"

"I've seen worse." Kelly pushed a portfolio across the table.

"He wants to schedule another shoot, of course?"

"Well, the whole team is under a bit of time pressure. The campaign's already running late because your trip to Europe pushed the shoot back, and your accident couldn't have come at a worse moment."

Erika reached for the portfolio. Inside were ten different photos, each larger than life-size. She flipped through them dispassionately and tossed the portfolio back on the table. The photos spilled out and slid across the slick surface. "Well, there's nothing outstanding in that batch. Tell him I sympathize, but unless he wants to photograph me in profile, it'll have to wait."

"He won't be very happy to hear that," Kelly warned. "He wanted to come himself—to reason with you, as he put it."

"About what? Has he convinced himself the cover story's true after all?"

"I told him your orders were that only I could visit."

"Great thinking, Kelly. Now he's probably convinced I'm just hiding out because I want a vacation. If he insists, let him come over—he can see for himself how impossible it is."

Amos pushed the photographs around as if he were arranging playing cards for a magic trick. "You're on to something there, Erika. A profile would at least stand out from the crowd. There's no major difference between these pictures and every other Ladylove ad in the last year." He pushed the photos aside with a fingertip.

"Continuity is an important factor in advertising," Erika pointed out.

"But sameness isn't. Why bother with another shoot when he could pull a photo from the last one, use a computer program to change the color of your collar, put on the tag line of the month, and run with it? Nobody would know the difference."

"Of course they would. There are subtle distinctions—"

"Distinctions the public never notices."

"They may not realize it, but at some level they— Wait a minute. How would you happen to know what every Ladylove ad in the last year has looked like?"

Amos raised an eyebrow. "My dear, everybody in the western world knows what Ladylove ads look like. Your face is everywhere."

"Well, yes," she admitted. "But why would you have paid special attention to a cosmetics company's ads? It's not exactly a product that a guy would have reason to notice, like if we were selling car insurance or computers or racquetball equipment."

"Racquetball." Amos's voice was wistful, and he drew the word out as if it were a lover's name. "You realize, of course, that it's cruel to remind me that I'm missing out on racquetball, shut up here.''

"Yeah, well, I'm missing out on my exercise routine, too.'' Erika refused to be distracted. "Are you some kind of advertising genius? One of those guys who makes a whole career out of studying advertising campaigns and telling the company everything they're doing wrong?''

She realized, just a little too late, that Kelly was giving her a very odd look, but it took her an instant to figure out why her assistant was acting so puzzled.

When it hit her, it seemed so obvious that she was embarrassed. Kelly was startled not because of the question but because it was Erika who was asking it.

And once she stopped to think it over, it did seem to be the kind of thing she should have already known about Amos—what exactly it was that he had done for a living, before he'd decided to write a book. She'd married the man, after all. It looked a bit odd not to know the basics.

Come to think of it, though, what *had* he been doing? She didn't even know for certain how old he was. Past thirty, surely—which meant he must have been knocking around the world for a few years.

Unless he'd been living with his parents, who might have gotten annoyed at his lack of progress on the book, so they'd finally thrown him out—and that was why he'd taken the job as Stephen's assistant.

Maybe you're the one who should be writing fiction, Erika told herself.

"Never mind,'' she said briskly. "Kelly, I'm going to go read this contract so I don't keep you waiting any longer than necessary.''

"Fresh coffee to take with you?'' Amos asked. He picked up her cup and went to refill it.

"Take your time," Kelly said. "I can send a courier over this afternoon to pick up the papers."

Erika shook her head. "No matter how good the courier service is, I'd rather know exactly who's got possession of them. The last thing we need is for the *Sentinel* to get a copy. Enjoy your breakfast—it won't take me long."

She picked up the legal folder and headed almost automatically for the den. As she left the kitchen she heard Kelly ask, "Let me guess. You're really working for some new ad agency that's trying to get Ladylove's business."

Erika couldn't help it. She paused in midstep to listen for the answer.

"And I married Erika just so I could whisper new ad slogans into her ear while she sleeps," Amos said. "You know—subliminal suggestion and hypnosis, so that one of these mornings she'll wake up convinced to hire my firm."

Erika recognized the tone of voice—matter-of-fact and absolutely saintly—and she could picture the cherubic expression which always accompanied it. In short, he was lying his head off. She just hoped Kelly was getting the full effect.

His tone became brisk. "Sorry to disappoint you, Kelly. I wish I was a hotshot, because Ladylove could use one."

Now that, Erika was certain, was the truth. She just wasn't quite sure whether or not to feel relieved. She was glad to know that her original suspicion had been wrong— that Amos wasn't something more than he'd seemed, and that he hadn't had hidden motives for watching her.

Yet if he was telling the truth about being no more than a casual viewer of Ladylove's ads—well, that part wasn't exactly comforting. If from his random, chance exposure, he thought all the company's ads looked alike, then many of their target customers probably had the same impression.

And if the public perception was that all the ads were the same...

"Then we might as well stop wasting money on producing new ones, and just rerun the old set," Erika muttered.

She'd definitely have to think about that one. *But not today,* she told herself. *You have more important concerns to deal with today.*

The door of the den stood open, and Amos's computer was humming on the desk. He must have been at work already this morning when Kelly arrived. He'd been gone long enough, however, that the screen had gone black rather than displaying whatever he'd been working on when the doorbell rang.

It was probably just as well, Erika thought, that the computer had put itself to sleep so she wouldn't be tempted to snitch on her promise. She'd given her pledge not to read his first draft, but it would have been almighty difficult to look at a screen full of words and keep herself from reading even a sentence or two. And to read a bit and then pretend that she hadn't would be dishonest. Perhaps even more to the point, it might prove impossible.

Because what if she read half a page and hated it? There was no guaranteeing that just because she liked Amos, she'd also like his work.

No, it was much better not to have any idea what he was writing. Then she wouldn't have to pretend not to have any idea what his novel was about. Because even though the odds were that she'd like it—

Because you like Amos, you'd probably like his work.

Now that was odd. She'd never thought about it quite that way before. In fact, whether or not she liked him had never entered into the equation. He'd been a means to an end, that was all, and if she'd had to rank her feelings about him on a scale, she'd have said they fell somewhere be-tween indifference and aggravation. He certainly wasn't someone she would have chosen as a friend—he was noth-ing like Stephen, who was easy and predictable and calm-ing to be around.

Of course, she hadn't exactly been looking for a friend. She'd needed someone who was presentable, believable and anonymous enough to be of no interest to the tabloids.

And for sale, a little voice at the back of her brain re-minded. *Don't forget that part. He never would have been interested in you if it wasn't for the money.*

"And that's just fine with me," Erika said firmly. Still, she was fortunate to find, since they had been thrown to-gether, that she didn't actively dislike him after all. This would all have been much more difficult if they'd despised each other.

When Erika came back into the kitchen, Kelly's plate had been pushed aside and she was sitting with elbows on the table and her cup cradled in her hands. "I've been at Ladylove for about three years," she said. "I was hired to be Erika's personal assistant on the first photo shoots she did. You know, just a warm body to run for a comb or a water bottle, so she didn't have to leave the set. Then when she took over in the head office, she wanted someone she could trust…"

"Having a nice chat?" Erika laid the folder on the table.

Kelly looked up, eyes wide.

Obviously, Erika thought, she'd been so engrossed in the conversation that she hadn't even heard her boss come in. And just as obviously, something was different now than it had been before, because Kelly hadn't reacted this way the first time Erika appeared. She'd even been encouraging Amos to come and get Erika, while now…

She looks nervous. As if she's been caught doing some-thing she shouldn't.

Well, that answer was obvious, Erika thought. Kelly was flirting with Amos, and she was afraid that Erika would be angry. What a shame it was that she couldn't just tell Kelly to enjoy herself—because despite the entanglements of the moment, Amos was free for the taking.

But she couldn't say it. What was it Amos had said about Stephen? Something about being much more convincing when he issued a denial because he wasn't lying. The same went for Kelly, of course.

If Felix liked the deal he was being offered, then Kelly—and everyone else in New York City—would know before long that Amos was a free agent. But in the meantime...

"How was the contract?" Kelly asked.

Erika had to pull her thoughts back to the subject. "I made a few margin notes for the lawyers to look at. But I think with those things cleared up, we can send it over to Felix and see what he says."

"That sounds like cause for celebration," Amos said.

It was no surprise to Erika that he was looking forward to freedom. She shook her head. "Not just yet. It's only a preliminary offer, so the negotiations could still have a very long way to go." She moved around the kitchen island to pour herself another cup of coffee.

Kelly stood up, smoothing her skirt. "I'll get the process started. It was nice talking to you, Amos."

But she didn't seem to be in any hurry to leave, for Erika could hear their voices by the front door for several minutes.

When Amos came back to the kitchen, Erika was a little startled. "I thought you'd be going straight to work."

"Sorry to intrude on you."

"No, I just meant... You're not intruding." *I'm just surprised you came back.*

"I wanted another cup of coffee to take with me."

Of course he hadn't come to talk to her. "I just poured the last cup for myself, but I'll make another pot."

She expected that he'd leave then, but instead Amos leaned against the island and watched while she filled the coffeemaker and plugged it in.

The scrutiny made her nervous. "I'll bring you a cup when it's done," she offered finally. "It's no trouble—it's not like I have a lot of things to occupy my time."

Still he didn't move. "What are you going to do today?"

"I don't know. It's very quiet here in the daytime, isn't it?"

"Up here it seems to be," he said dryly. "Downstairs was another story."

"Well, yes. I don't quite know what to do with myself."

"How long has it been since you've had a week away from the office?"

"You mean when I haven't been traveling for the company?"

"That answers my question." He cleared Kelly's plate off the table and put it in the dishwasher. "Doesn't your phone ever ring?"

"Not often. Most of my calls go to the office."

"But right now people must be wondering how you are."

"Remember? Officially, nothing happened. I'm just on my honeymoon."

"Ah, yes. I'd almost forgotten. It's funny what sleeping alone on your wedding night will do to one's memory." He moved closer, raising a hand to gently push her hair back from her temple to inspect the bruise. "It's looking a little better than I expected. But I do have to say that particular shade of purple isn't really your color.''

"It was your idea not to even try to cover it up," she said almost defensively. ''In case it'll heal faster.''

He didn't move his hand away. "Does it bother you when I look?"

"Not really," she lied. "I can't judge it myself—it's hard to see the whole effect in a mirror.''

So if it doesn't bother you, Erika, why can't you stand still? she asked herself.

"Besides," she said, "it's not like we're dating or anything.''

"No, we're just on our honeymoon." His voice was dry. "Out of curiosity, Erika, how long has it been since a guy's seen you without makeup?"

She considered. "You mean besides the artists who do my face for the photo shoots? I don't really remember. I was about twelve when my father took me to Ladylove's headquarters so they could give me lessons, and after that—''

"Whew. Getting formal instruction must have taken all the fun out of being a little girl and playing dress-up with your mother's lipstick.''

"*Nobody* touched my mother's lipstick." She dumped the dregs of her coffee and rinsed her cup with warm water, so she didn't have to look at him. "Do you like Kelly?"

"She seems very pleasant.''

Erika hadn't exactly expected him to be effusive, but his guarded tone and the fact that he'd waited just a second too long to answer startled her. That sort of caution could only mean one thing—he really liked Kelly, but he didn't want to admit it to Erika.

Not that she could blame him—but it didn't matter to her. They were both nice people, and she'd be pleased to see them get together eventually, if that was the way things worked out.

Absolutely thrilled, in fact, she told herself. *No question about it.*

Erika had been right—the apartment was very quiet. *Too quiet,* Amos thought. Unnaturally quiet. It was, in fact, just short of silent-as-the-grave quiet.

He didn't count the muted hum of traffic from far below, because that was nothing more than white noise at this distance. And he didn't count the occasional cycle of the heating system, either. What he was listening for—and it annoyed the hell out of him when he realized it—was Erika.

He knew she was there, somewhere inside the four walls of the apartment, because she couldn't possibly be anywhere else. She had agreed to stay under cover for Ladylove's sake, and he didn't doubt that she'd do what she said she would. But even if it hadn't been for her promise, he didn't think she'd be eager to go out. That was a beauty of a black eye, one that no woman would be eager to show off. Especially not a woman whose face was such a crucial part of her work and her identity.

The thing that had really surprised him was when she'd walked into the kitchen this morning wearing no makeup at all. Even though she didn't seem to be nearly as vain as he would have expected the Face of Ladylove to be, he would never have guessed that she would present herself to the world without the mask that cosmetics provided.

Not that she needed the help of makeup. The dark bruise on the side of her face only served to accent the porcelain perfection of the rest of her skin.

And, of course, she hadn't intended to face the whole world, or even Kelly. Only Amos. And she'd made it quite plain that where she was concerned, Amos didn't count.

It's not like we're dating or anything, she'd said. He wondered if she had any idea how naive that had sounded.

Naive—maybe, he told himself. *But true. And a guy with any smarts at all wouldn't forget it.*

He shifted uncomfortably in the desk chair. It was a little too small for him, intended more for someone Erika's size. Though she was tall for a woman, she was fine-boned and delicate...

How could she possibly be making no noise out there? The walls weren't thick enough to block every sound. This morning, he'd been able to hear the shower running in her bathroom before he'd even raised a hand to knock on her door.

What could she possibly be doing that was producing no sound at all?

Maybe if she was asleep...

But surely she shouldn't be sleepy. It wasn't even lunchtime yet, and she hadn't gotten up till late. Unless she'd lain awake last night, she shouldn't be short of sleep. Maybe the pain medication she'd taken yesterday was still affecting her. Or maybe the doctor had been wrong and she had a concussion after all. Maybe she was lying somewhere unconscious...

He'd been concentrating so hard on the lack of noise that when the crash echoed through the apartment, he almost believed that he'd imagined it. Even so, he was out of his chair and down the hall before he stopped to think, skidding to a halt on the threshold of the dining room.

Erika was standing next to the table, a wrapped package in her arms. Around her, on the floor, lay a tumbled pile of boxes, and she was looking at him with dismay flooding her eyes. He wondered how much of her consternation was because of the mess and how much was simply because he'd showed up.

At least now he knew why he hadn't been able to hear her until the crash. She was as far from the den as it was possible to be and still stay inside the apartment.

"What did you do?" he asked. "Just yank one out of the bottom of the stack?"

She gave him a look that made him feel singed along the edges. "Of course not. I do have a nodding acquaintance with the concept of gravity."

"Sorry." His voice felt gruff.

"It appears to me that the gentlemen who did the stacking weren't being careful. I quite understand why Stephen was in a hurry to get out of here in a hurry last night—but what's your excuse?"

Amos decided he'd just as soon not answer that, so he tried changing the subject. "Why were you messing with this, anyway?"

"I was trying to rearrange it all so the piles wouldn't collapse. Now I have to open everything to find out which one has the broken glass in it."

"Yeah, I thought I heard a kind of tinkle—" He swallowed the rest of the sentence. "I guess maybe I should help."

"Oh, not at all," she said pleasantly. "Go on back to work."

Of course she wanted him to go away. She'd tried to nudge him out of the kitchen the minute Kelly had left, and she'd been avoiding him ever since. It was enough to make a man feel ornery. "That's all right. The writing's not going very well this morning."

"What a shame," Erika said. The sarcasm in her voice was so delicate that if he hadn't expected it, the barb might have gone over his head entirely.

Amos started to pick up the fallen boxes, giving each

one an experimental shake. "What's the big deal? You were going to open all these anyway."

"As a matter of fact, I wasn't. The appropriate etiquette, if the marriage doesn't last, is to return the gifts—so I could hardly keep them, under the circumstances."

"But that won't be for a couple of months yet."

He could almost hear what she was thinking. *I devoutly hope it doesn't take that long.*

"So what are you getting at?" she said. "If you want to admire the loot, help yourself. Just set the damaged ones on the sideboard and I'll figure out how to get replacements."

Amos shook his head. "That's not what I mean. If I sent someone a wedding gift and it came back months later in the original wrapping, I'd suspect the bride knew all along that she'd be returning everything. You might as well call a press conference and announce that this marriage is a scam."

She looked, Amos thought, as if she were considering it. Now he was really starting to feel perverse.

"Come on, Erika. I'll open, you keep a list." He tore the glossy white paper off the first box and handed it to her. "Got a pen? This looks like…a stainless-steel bonsai tree."

Erika looked at the box. "There's no label, and no marking."

"You mean you don't know what it is, either? That's reassuring. I guess we'll deal with that one later." He set the tree back into the box and picked up the next package. "You know, honey, ever since last night when you brought up the subject of sleeping together—"

"I did not do anything of the sort."

"—I've been thinking, if we're going to make that demonstration for Stephen look convincing, a little practice would be a great idea.''

"Think again, Amos.'' She sounded perfectly calm.

''Things have changed a lot, you know. The original deal didn't say anything about spending twenty-four hours a day together.''

''I didn't ask you to come out of the den this morning.''

He ignored the interruption. ''And we didn't put in the agreement that I'd have to give up things like racquetball and stay inside all the time, either.''

''No, we didn't. However, since you refused to put anything in writing, Amos, it's just your word against mine what we agreed to.''

''Yes,'' he said softly. ''It is. Your word against mine.'' He waited and watched with satisfaction while it sank in on her that her own argument could be used against her with equal efficiency. Suddenly, Erika's eyes turned to wide, soft, violet pools of apprehension.

She would deny it, of course, but she was fascinated. He'd made definite progress. Now the question was how best to capitalize on it.

But one thing was damn sure, he thought. She wasn't going to be ignoring him anymore.

CHAPTER EIGHT

ERIKA didn't know how many times the phone had rung before the sound actually registered in her mind, but even when she heard it, she had trouble moving.

It was ridiculous, she told herself, to feel mesmerized by the way Amos was looking at her. And as for their agreement—well, she knew perfectly what they'd agreed to, and so did he, and she wasn't about to give in to blackmail at this late date.

"So what are you saying, Amos?" she asked briskly. "If I don't sleep with you, you'll talk? You know, it would serve you right if I agreed—because you're not really interested. I think you're only yanking my chain to entertain yourself, and it's not going to work." She handed him the scrap of wrapping paper and her pen and crossed the hallway to the kitchen to check who was calling.

By the time she came back, Amos had unwrapped another half dozen packages. "So your phone does actually ring," he said. "I was beginning to think it was so unlisted that even you didn't know the number. I found the broken glass, by the way. It looks like it used to be a—" He tipped his head to one side. "What's the matter? You're absolutely white."

"It was Kelly, on the phone." She swallowed hard. "Somebody who was at the photo shoot talked, and the *Sentinel's* running a story."

He set the package he was holding on the corner of the table. "Well, that solves a number of problems for you. For one thing, if everybody in the world knows you have

132

a black eye anyway, you might as well get dressed and go to work. That's what you wanted, isn't it?''

Her eyelids felt prickly. She wanted to nod, to agree, and then to run to her room. But she couldn't dodge this.

Tell him, Erika. You have to tell him the rest.

She took a deep breath. ''It's worse than that, Amos. They're saying that I didn't get the black eye by running into a light. The story says that you did it.''

There was a long silence.

''Kelly said it's very delicately phrased, but the implication's clear—you hit me and knocked me down.''

''And that bothers you?'' he said finally.

''Of course it bothers me. What do you expect?''

''Why?''

''You don't understand why I mind that the *Sentinel*'s saying you slugged me? What's the matter with you, Amos? It's not fair, that's why. You didn't do it and everybody who was there knows it.''

''Yes, they do. So—''

''It's one thing for the *Sentinel* to say nasty things about me. I'm used to it—they've been doing it for years. But to take after you...'' She dashed a fingertip under her eye to wipe away an inconvenient blur of tears. But she'd momentarily forgotten the bruise, and the pain of jabbing the tender flesh made the tears flow even faster. ''Damn.''

''Come here,'' Amos said. His voice sounded odd.

She didn't intend to do anything of the sort, but something about his tone drew her toward him. He pulled a handkerchief out of his pocket and gently blotted her tears. ''Thanks,'' she muttered.

''You're worried about me,'' he said.

Her tears welled up again. ''You didn't ask for this kind of treatment. And we can't even sue because they're always just careful enough about what they say.''

Amos folded her fingers around the handkerchief, then stooped and picked her up.

Startled, Erika struggled. "What are you—?"

"Careful. If I drop you, you'll have a bruise on your rear to match your eye, and then the *Sentinel* will really have a story."

He carried her around the corner into the living room, and sat down on the couch with her cradled on his lap. "Now you can go ahead and cry."

"You're just going to sit here and hold me while I sob?" she said skeptically.

"Why not? It's as good a place as any for me to think."

She refolded the handkerchief in an attempt to find a dry spot. "What are you thinking about?"

"That it's past time for someone to protect you."

"Like how?"

"I don't know yet. That's why I'm thinking."

She had no intention of giving in to tears. Shedding a few now and then was unavoidable, she supposed—it was just part of being a woman. But breaking down and sobbing was a weakness she didn't indulge.

It's past time for someone to protect you...

Not that she needed protection, and under ordinary circumstances she'd probably have laughed at the idea. But it was a pretty sentiment—it made her feel warm and cherished—and she was already feeling emotional. Suddenly she couldn't hold back any longer. She put her head down on his shoulder and let the tears flow.

Amos's hand cupped her head, stroking her hair. She was crying too hard to hear what he was saying, except to know that his voice was low and soothing. He might have been comforting a crabby infant... The thought mortified her, and she told herself to straighten up.

"Finished already?" he said. "That didn't take long.

You hit on something a bit ago, when you said everybody who was at the photo shoot knows I didn't hit you. So where did the *Sentinel* get the story?''

Erika shrugged. ''Made it up, I suppose. Or they offered someone enough money to tell them what they wanted to hear. That's probably more likely, because then they can say that they didn't intend to cause harm, they just made a mistake.''

''Your marketing and advertising and PR people might learn a lesson from this,'' he mused, ''about how foolish it is to tell lies when the truth would serve them better.''

''Oh, they'll learn it,'' Erika said grimly. ''Or they won't be working for me anymore.''

He pulled back a bit and looked at her. ''I'd suggest you wait till the tears are dry before you lay down the law to them.''

She bit her lip. ''I suppose I'm all blotchy.'' *When beautiful women cry, they're not beautiful anymore,* her father's voice whispered in the back of her mind.

''Not too bad, actually. It sort of balances out the bruise.'' He stroked her hair.

''What are we going to do, Amos?''

''That depends on whether Kelly actually saw the story or just heard about it.''

''She heard about it, I think—the paper won't hit the street till late this afternoon. What difference does it make?''

''Because we don't really know what's in it. The people at the *Sentinel* might be cunning enough to float a rumor past Kelly just to see if they can get a reaction from you—without running a story at all.''

''Possible,'' Erika conceded. ''But they've never done anything like that before.''

''Nevertheless, we're not doing anything until we see

what the story really says. Then we'll decide what to do. It'll be okay, Erika.''

His hand was warm against her hair, and she felt his lips brush against her uninjured temple. The touch was soothing, and she closed her eyes and relaxed against him. She didn't know whether it was because of his warmth, or the comfort of being held, or the relief she felt that he wasn't angry, but she was feeling almost sleepy.

"Amos?'' She yawned. "Thanks for not being mad at me for dragging you into this. Getting you a reputation as a wife-beater and all.''

"Don't give it a thought, sweetheart. Heck, in certain circles, that would just increase my macho appeal.''

"Yeah, the redhead down the hall will be thrilled to find out that you're not only a writer but a caveman. The combination would probably be like an aphrodisiac for her.''

"I'll have to try that out,'' Amos murmured.

Erika turned to look at him, eyes narrowed. "I thought you weren't attracted to her.''

"I'm not.'' He cupped her chin in his palm. "I just said I'd try out the idea.'' He nibbled at her lower lip for an instant, and then kissed her, long and softly.

It would hardly be polite of her to make a fuss about a mere kiss, Erika thought, when he'd been such a good sport about something which was much more important. One kiss…there was no big deal about one gentle, companionable, friendly, sympathetic kiss, as long as nobody took it seriously. And she intended to make absolutely certain of that.

So she kissed him back, just as gently. And when he raised his head, she said, "If that's what you call being a caveman—''

Amos smiled and his arms tightened around her. "Oh,

that was just the beginning of the experiment,'' he said softly.

Erika felt her insides jumble around as if he'd given her a good shaking. ''I was only teasing,'' she tried to say, but her voice didn't seem to be working quite right, and in any case, her words were smothered against his mouth as he kissed her again.

There was nothing tender, nothing delicate, about this kiss. But there was nothing Neanderthal about it, either. He was holding her closely, but there was no force in his grip—she could have broken free if she'd wanted to.

She just didn't want to.

He was fierce and tender in turns, shifting so quickly that she couldn't get her breath, much less predict what he might do next. All she could do was react, and even then she was at a disadvantage because her reflexes seemed to have slowed. When he gathered her up in his arms once more and strode across the hall toward her bedroom, she was too stunned even to struggle.

''This is getting out of hand,'' she managed to say. To her own ears, her voice sounded like a half-tuned radio. ''I didn't mean—''

He carried her into her room and laid her almost reverently on the bed. She tried to roll away—at least, she told herself she was trying to roll away. And she'd have done it, too, if she hadn't been so out of breath that it was impossible to move.

''Take a nap,'' Amos said. ''I'm going back to work.''

Erika couldn't believe her ears. ''You were thinking about your *book?*''

He turned in the doorway. ''You see,'' he said, sounding almost apologetic, ''it was a love scene that was giving me problems, and I think I've figured it out now. Thanks for helping.''

She picked up the first object she touched—the vampire novel she'd gotten at the literacy banquet—and threw it at him.

Amos fielded it neatly and brought it back to her. "If you've been staying up all night reading this, no wonder you're yawning."

She clutched the book to her chest and muttered, "So much for you being a caveman."

His eyes had turned an odd smoky blue. "I'm the breed of caveman who likes his cavewomen to be every bit as interested as I am."

Cavewomen, plural. That figures.

"I'll wait till you're ready, Erika."

"You'll be waiting a long time." She opened the book and pretended to study the first page. *I knew he was bluffing about wanting to sleep with me,* she told herself. *And that's the way I want it.*

"Don't underestimate me, sweetheart. Or yourself." Amos closed the door behind him with a soft little click.

To Erika's surprise, she actually got involved in the tale of vampires who wintered at a spa near the Arctic Circle where one of the chief attractions was a world class blood cellar with the equivalent of a wine list—sectioned off by type, cross-match, and IQ level of the donor rather than by vineyard and year.

Every few minutes, of course, the threat of the *Sentinel* story floated back into her mind. But there was nothing she could do about it at the moment, so she pushed it aside and returned to Stakeout, Alaska. Maybe Amos was right—the editors were simply putting up a trial balloon to see whether she'd react. She'd know soon enough whether the story was real.

By the time she finished the book, it was late afternoon

and Amos was in the living room. As she came in he poured a glass of sherry from the wet bar and handed it to her.

Be casual, she told herself. So what if he'd kissed her so thoroughly that her lips still felt swollen? It hadn't meant anything to him. And it didn't to her, either. Not really. "You've been quiet all afternoon. Did you get your love scene worked out?"

His eyes sparkled. "Not quite yet. But it's developing nicely, thanks to you."

"Glad I could help." She pointed to the coffee table. "Is that the *Sentinel?*"

He nodded. "Stephen brought it up a few minutes ago. Kelly had the scoop right."

Her heart sank. She'd really been hoping that it had been nothing more than an attempt to smoke her out. When she read the story, she felt even worse. There was a sly, gleeful, almost sneering note about it. Even the *Sentinel* hadn't taken this tone before.

Amos watched as she read, and then said in a matter-of-fact voice, "I particularly like their suggestion that you owe it to your public to show yourself to prove you're not being battered."

"It's almost a challenge, isn't it? What are we going to do, Amos? If I stay hidden, they'll take it as confirmation— it would be like admitting they're right. But if I show up in public, it'll actually be confirmation—or at least it'll look that way—and that would be even worse."

"If you go out, my reputation will be in shreds, and if you stay in, they'll go after both of us."

"That's about the size of it." She drained her sherry and held out her glass for a refill. "I suppose we could have Kelly announce that we've slipped off to Europe for a week, but I hardly think that will stop them."

Amos shook his head. "Nope. We're going to face it head-on. We have dinner reservations tonight at the Civic Club."

Erika gasped. "Have you gone mad? You want me to go out for dinner looking like this?"

"Of course not, darling." His voice was soothing.

"That's good. What's the plan, then? You've found a double for me?"

"With a face as distinctive as yours, and a zillion photographs floating around, there's no such thing as a stand-in. We'd never get by with it. Stephen's downtown right now getting you a very wide-brimmed hat with a black veil. I hope you have a dress it will go nicely with."

She was ready to shriek. "Amos, I told you long ago that a hat is no good. I never wear hats—I'd look suspicious in a hat even if there was nothing wrong with my face. And hiding behind a veil is going to do nothing but make people ask more questions."

"Exactly. Let's go look through your closet. Stephen suggested your black cocktail dress with the sequins, but I want to see what the other choices are before we decide."

"What are you thinking, Amos? This is crazy!"

He strolled across to her bedroom, apparently paying no attention to her protest.

Erika, with no good option left, followed.

Amos pulled the closet doors open and flicked through the hangers and dress bags. Then he turned on the lights above her dressing table and pulled out the bench, inviting her to sit.

She shook her head. "Not till you tell me what you're intending to do."

"I'm thinking," he said, "that you were right about the caveman stuff. It might even be fun. Let's try it out, shall we?"

*   *   *

The Civic Club was always busy, but Erika had never before seen it as crowded on a Thursday evening as it was when they got out of the cab by the main entrance. Her hat barely fit through the door of the cab, and the instant she was out in the open, the crisp breeze caught at the brim and threatened to tear her veil away. "I feel like I'm wearing a cartwheel on my head," she muttered. "And if I'm not careful, that's what I'll be doing—cartwheels all the way down the street." She slapped one hand atop her head to keep the hat in place. Her long black cape whipped in the wind.

Amos tipped the cabbie and offered her his arm. Erika looked at him what she hoped would appear to be fond exasperation and switched hands so she would have the correct one free to tuck into the bend of his elbow. "Where did Stephen find this abominable hat, anyway?" she asked.

"He didn't say. It's no doubt one of the secrets he doesn't share with just everyone."

"And for good reason. If I knew where the place was, I'd be tempted to burn it down." Inside, she slid carefully out of the cape so she didn't lose the featherweight wool shawl draped around her shoulders. She tucked the unusually large evening bag she was carrying under her arm, straightened her delicate black gloves, and shook her head with true regret when the cloakroom attendant offered to take the hat.

Amos handed his coat to the attendant, straightened the sleeves of his tuxedo, and solicitously helped pull the shawl tighter over Erika's shoulders. "That should do it. Nothing's showing."

"This is insane, you know. It's not going to work."

Amos sounded unconcerned. "We'll find out how good

a performer you are. Just think, darling—if you can pull this off, you might have a future in acting as well as modeling.''

"I just want to go back to running my company."

"This is the fastest route back to your office." He looked around the rotunda and gazed up for a minute at the arched and frescoed ceiling far overhead. "Nice place. Not my usual style, of course."

Erika rolled her eyes. "Just remember what I told you about the forks, all right? When in doubt, work from the outside in."

"I'll just do what you do. People will notice that I can't take my eyes off you, of course, but they'll think it's because I'm in love."

"More likely they'll suspect you're trying to prevent me from escaping you or calling for help. This way." She bypassed the lounge and headed straight for the dining room.

When the maître d' first laid eyes on Erika's hat, he looked for a split second like a bird confronted with a cobra—half-horrified, half-fascinated, and completely paralyzed. But like all of his kind, his job was to pretend not to notice the eccentricities of his customers, and he quickly reclaimed his composure. "This way, Ms. Forrester. Sir. Your table is ready."

He led them through the very center of the dining room to a quieter corner and a small round table for two. Instead of chairs, there was a black leather banquette couch which curved around the table. Erika had seen the setup a hundred times, but she'd never paid much attention before. Tonight, it seemed to shout that it was a table meant for lovers.

She slid in behind the table, and Amos joined her, sitting very close. Her heartbeat had already speeded up a little, and as his thigh pressed against hers it seemed to kick into overdrive. *All part of the plan,* she reminded herself.

She let her gaze sweep once across the dining room, trying to see in a single glance who was present, and then focused on Amos. "I don't remember this table being quite so exposed," she said.

"Really? Use it a lot, do you?"

"No. I mean—well, of course I've had dates here."

He reached for her hand and brought it to his mouth. Even through the lightweight glove, Erika could feel the warmth of his breath as he nibbled at her knuckles.

"Stephen bribed them to move some of the plants away," Amos said. "Not all of them, of course, because that would look obvious. Just enough to make the table the center of attention."

"I think my first really big mistake was suggesting that you learn to appreciate having Stephen around."

"Now, darling, don't be so tart-tongued. What are you going to eat tonight?"

She opened the leather-bound folder which held the menu and almost automatically tried to brush away the veil so she could read the fine print.

As if it wasn't bad enough that the veil was black and closely woven, Stephen had chosen one which sported little embroidered dots at regular intervals. No wonder she was seeing spots, Erika thought irritably. They were really there.

"Certainly not lobster," she said. "It's hard enough to deal with a bib, but impossible to eat with a veil as well. I'll try the filet mignon, I think."

The wine steward and the waiter approached, and Amos negotiated the rituals of ordering and wine-tasting with apparent ease. As the two men left the table, Erika relaxed—imperceptibly, she hoped. But Amos didn't miss much. Of course, with her glued to his side like that, there wasn't much chance that he'd overlook so much as a shiver.

He looked down at her with the sparkle of mischief that

she'd come to recognize. "Stephen taught me. Did you really read the vampire book, or were you just in your room this afternoon pouting because I'd left you alone?"

"I certainly wasn't pouting." She raised her wineglass, realized that it was on the wrong side of the veil, sighed, and set it down again without a taste. "I can see this becoming a whole new diet fad," she muttered. "Yes, I read the book. It actually wasn't bad."

"Would you like to tell me the plot? It'll give us something to talk about. In fact, it will probably get us all the way through appetizers and into the main course, depending on how many people table-hop over here to try to find out what's going on."

"And all you'll have to do to keep the conversation going is hang on my every word and look fascinated while I do all the work."

"Hey, listening to a vampire story isn't going to be easy. You seriously liked it?"

"I'm afraid so." Erika sighed. "I suppose that means my mind's deteriorating. By the time I get back to work I probably won't be able to understand a balance sheet. But I'd feel really silly telling you a vampire story when you've ordered a steak cooked medium rare. I could summarize the mystery, if you like. Only—come to think of it—that's a bit bloody, too."

He raised his eyebrows. "You've read it as well? I hadn't even noticed it was gone. When have you had time?"

"Last night. I'm sorry—I suppose I should have asked permission to take it, since it belongs to you."

He shrugged. "You're the one who paid for the tickets. So you couldn't sleep last night? That's interesting. Were you worried that I'd misinterpret your offer to demonstrate for Stephen?"

There were moments, Erika thought, when a veil wasn't so bad after all. Like when a slip of the tongue left her feeling a bit pink and embarrassed. It had been bad enough when she'd made that stupid remark in the first place. But to admit to him that the whole thing had kept her awake half the night...

A shadow fell across the table, and she looked up to see a matron standing there. Amos half-rose, but the woman waved him back into his seat. "Erika," she demanded, "introduce me to your new husband."

Erika went through the mechanics, but the woman barely spared Amos a glance. She was too busy trying to get a good look through the veil. Stephen had carried out his commission well, however, and the matron had to admit defeat and go away. But she spent the next half hour whispering to her dinner companions, and now and then one of them pointed in Erika's direction.

After the first dozen visitors, Erika stopped trying to keep count. Only a few stuck out from the crowd. One was the debutante who said, "Aren't you two a symphony in black and blue tonight. Oh, dear—I meant black and white. I'm so sorry."

Another standout was the couple who had sat next to them at the literacy banquet and exclaimed over Erika's diamond ring. Tonight the wife seemed distracted, hardly following the conversation because she was so obviously concerned about Erika, and the husband seemed on the verge of taking a swing at Amos.

"I hope they're not in a hurry to leave," Erika said as the couple went back to their own table. "I'd hate for them to miss the show."

"How much longer?"

"Very soon. The *Sentinel*'s photographer is over in that far corner, shooting with a telephoto lens."

"I don't see anybody."

"Of course not. He's one of the pros—no glaring flash, no getting in someone's face. Everybody here has had time to notice and stare and speculate, and to talk over the *Sentinel* story. And a good many of the people here are on their way to the theater, so just about the time their dessert is served, I'll give them something to talk about for the rest of the evening."

"Well, I see flames on a silver cart across the room. It looks like they're starting to barbecue bananas. You're on, kid."

Erika pushed her plate away. Her steak was cold because of all the interruptions. Not that she'd felt like eating in the first place.

She moved her oversize evening bag into her lap, unzipped it and made sure that the object she needed was right on top. Then she gripped the wide brim of her hat with both hands.

A sudden hush fell over the dining room. Heads turned, and a few chairs scraped as people moved to get a better view. At several tables she saw diners elbowing the people on each side.

"I feel like a stripper," she muttered.

"Do you have a lot of these fantasies? Because I'd much rather hear about them than the plots of books." Amos sipped his wine.

Erika lifted the hat off and set it on the table. As she moved, the fine wool shawl slid with a soft whoosh onto the floor, leaving her shoulders bare.

The dining room seemed much brighter without the veil shielding her eyes. Which meant, of course, that everyone there could see her clearly now, too. They could see not only the bruise and black eye on the right side of her face— the real one—but they had just as good a view of all the others. The yellowing stain on her jaw, the blue smudge near her collarbone just below where the shawl had rested, the reddish-purple marks on both upper arms where it appeared a hand had gripped so tightly that every finger had left a bruise.

The instant of dead, shocked silence gave way to gasps and then to murmurs—of astonishment, of horror, of anger. The man who'd been at the literacy banquet was on his feet, fists clenched.

"Damn, you're good," Amos said under his breath. "I'm tempted to confess. Get rid of them quick, before every man in the place gangs up to teach me a lesson."

Erika paused. "Come to think of it, now would be a great time to negotiate a little change in terms. Amos darling—"

His eyes went wide. "Erika. Sweetheart."

Amos Abernathy pleading...now that was a sight she wouldn't soon forget. Too bad she couldn't enjoy it for long. The crowd was, indeed, getting restive.

She stood up, looking around the room so everyone—including the photographer in the back corner—could get the full effect of the best makeup job she'd ever done. "I'm sure you've all heard about the story in today's *Sentinel*," she announced. "And you know, of course, that the *Sentinel* never gets anything wrong. They've said I'm an abused wife—so I must be an abused wife. Let me show you just how abused I am."

She pulled a cold-cream-soaked sponge out of her evening bag. With one swift wipe, the yellow stain on her jaw disappeared.

The crowd was still goggling at her, obviously confused.

She removed the bruised fingermarks on one arm and held up the stained sponge.

Now the shock had turned to laughter, and a few people

were applauding. "Serves them right," one woman said. "The things they say in that paper—awful, just awful. I'm glad to see them embarrassed for a change."

"Time for the getaway," Amos muttered.

Erika took a theatrical bow. "Now, if you'll excuse me, I think I'll go home to remove the rest," she announced.

The crowd rushed them, and it took fifteen minutes just to work their way through the dining room and retrieve their wraps from the cloakroom attendant. Erika was trying not to laugh. "I'll still have to give up my membership," she said breathlessly. "Causing two embarrassing scenes in a week—I'll be hearing from the board of governors any minute. But it was worth it."

Amos held her cape. "Did you see the look on the photographer's face when the marks started to disappear? I hope he doesn't try to sell those shots to the *Sentinel*."

A low voice behind Erika said, "I'm delighted, of course, to hear the rumors aren't true."

She swung around. "Felix! I didn't see you in the dining room."

"Unlike you, I prefer the quiet corners. I'm glad to run into you, because it saves me a phone call. I hate to intrude on your honeymoon any more than necessary."

"Intrude?" Erika said slowly.

"Yes. Now that I've read the purchase contract you've proposed, I'd like to arrange a meeting to talk about the details. Shall we say my office, tomorrow?"

Erika's throat closed up.

Amos's plan had worked, and the *Sentinel* would be silenced—at least for a while. But the success of the plan depended on the public believing that every last one of the bruises she'd displayed tonight were fake. Which meant she couldn't be seen tomorrow with a black eye.

"Tomorrow doesn't work for me," she said. "Let's try for sometime next week. I'll be back in the office then."

Felix tipped his head back and stared down his nose at her. "How badly do you want to put together this deal?" he asked softly.

I'm not backing out now, that's for sure. Not with everything I've already invested to make this work.

She scrambled for an alternative that would satisfy him. If she didn't have to run the gauntlet of an office building full of people...if it was only Felix she had to face... "How about my apartment? Dinner, tomorrow evening."

Felix was still watching her. "You want to meet with me privately."

"Yes," she said firmly. "It'll be much easier to work out the details between ourselves, and then we can let the lawyers figure out the final language. If we let them get involved in the fine points, we'll be forever getting anything decided."

"Quite true," Felix said slowly. "But there's a lot to cover. How about coming to my country house for the weekend? I'm afraid it's just a small place, not very exciting—no staff to speak of, and no entertainment. But we could get quite a lot accomplished..." His gaze flicked across Erika and rested for a moment on Amos. "The three of us."

Erika said, "I'm not sure Amos will be able—"

Felix lifted an eyebrow. "But he must come. I wouldn't dream of separating the newlyweds. I'll send a car for you tomorrow about five." Without waiting for an answer, he turned back toward the dining room.

The Civic Club's doorman hailed a cab for them, and Erika sank into the back seat, chewing on her bottom lip. "Now what? I'm really sorry, Amos. I tried to get you out of it, but—"

"Yes, I noticed that."

"Meaning what? You think I want to go by myself? Hardly." She put a pleading hand on his sleeve. "I'm going to need all the backup I can get. I've got to have you, Amos."

The words seemed to echo in the cab, and in her head. *I've got to have you, Amos.* And the essential truth which lay beneath the words struck her like a hammer blow.

Oh, no, she thought. *No. This can't be happening.*

Because she would not—absolutely could not—have fallen in love with him.

CHAPTER NINE

AN HOUR ago, Erika would have said such a thing was inconceivable. The mere idea of falling in love with Amos was laughable. Impossible.

But perhaps it was no wonder that she hadn't seen the picture which was forming. She'd been looking at the jigsaw puzzle from the back side, where everything was uniformly gray. But just now one seemingly careless comment had flipped the puzzle over in her mind. Suddenly she was looking at things from an entirely new angle. The colors had meshed into an image, and the pieces fit together too neatly to be denied.

The suggestion that she'd fallen in love with him accounted for everything—and it was the only explanation which did.

For instance, there was the way she'd felt so comforted this afternoon by a kiss and a cuddle that she'd gone off to take a nap, simply because Amos had told her things would work out all right. What else could possibly explain that reaction?

And take the uneasiness she'd felt whenever he mentioned sleeping together—it hadn't been distress she was feeling, or annoyance at him for harassing her. It had been a sneaky, teasing kind of anticipation.

Then throw in the edginess she'd experienced when he'd stood at the front door talking to Kelly. Erika hadn't been trying to convince herself that the two of them would make a good pair. Down deep inside, she'd been suffering from twinges of good old-fashioned jealousy.

And consider the protectiveness she'd felt when Kelly told her about the tabloid's accusations. There was no other reason for her to have been so defensive about Amos's reputation.

And then there was the sensation she'd had when Amos had disappeared for a moment at the literacy banquet and then turned up again carrying a diamond ring. Simply recalling how she'd felt in that instant—as if she'd been punched—was like being back there in the ballroom again. He had remembered that she needed a ring, when even she—the creator of the scheme—had forgotten it. And like a stage magician, he'd managed to produce one at the very instant when it had the most impact. She'd thought that what she was feeling was awed respect for the man's foresightedness and timing. But even then, something more had been creeping up on her.

She looked down at the diamond on her finger and the wedding ring nestled beside it. *Magic...* No, she corrected. There was nothing magical about the ring. It was a stage prop—that was all.

It was all fake. She had set the entire situation up that way, on purpose. But somewhere along the way, she had changed her mind about what she wanted.

Too bad, she told herself bleakly. *You can't switch rules in the middle of the game.*

Amos's voice broke through her reverie. "What's the matter, Erika?"

She blinked and tried to remember what they'd been talking about. What was it that had sent her off on this tangent? Oh, yes—Felix.

"I need you," she said. "Even if Felix only half-believes that this marriage is real, I can't take the chance of someone else wondering why I'm going off for a weekend on my own just days after the wedding. Besides, I've still got a black eye. If I'm going to carry that off with any style, I need your support—"

"Erika," he said softly. "I told you I'd go."

She must have been so topsy-turvy over her own epiphany that she hadn't even been listening to him. "Oh," she said lamely. "I guess I didn't hear you." She was once more momentarily glad of the veil, because it helped to hide the pink she felt rising in her cheeks.

The cab pulled up in front of the apartment building. This time she didn't care whether she injured the hat, so Erika bent the brim to make it easier to get through the car door, and paused to readjust the veil. She needn't have bothered, however, for though it wasn't late, the lobby was deserted.

Erika was glad Stephen wasn't still on duty, for she didn't want to rehash the evening's events. All she wanted was to reach her own bedroom and seek oblivion. Tomorrow things would look better.

If she had any luck at all, she told herself, by tomorrow she might even be able to convince herself that this sudden insight wasn't truth but only a brainstorm—that she hadn't fallen in love after all but had only been reacting to the stress of the evening and the euphoria of success.

What did she know about love, anyway? She'd thought she loved Denby Miles once, and look how that had turned out. Maybe she was wrong this time, too.

Come to think of it, her feelings about Amos were nothing like what she'd experienced with Denby. But did that fact make it more or less likely that this was real? Shouldn't being in love feel romantic? Soft and cuddly? Warm and delightful? *Fun?*

So maybe this wasn't love, since the main emotions she felt for Amos included exasperation, wariness, and a constant need to be on her toes lest he get ahead of her.

Shouldn't being in love make a woman feel like dancing, all light and happy and glorious?

Erika didn't feel like dancing. Quite the contrary. She felt as if her body was being pushed downward, her spine compressing—because it seemed to her that the cartwheel hat had suddenly taken on the weight as well as the dimensions of a flying saucer.

Once in the safety of the elevator she tugged the hat off, set it on her index fingertip, and gave it a spin. "I think I'll give this a toss off the balcony," she said.

"Better wait to see whether you need it again," Amos advised. "Stephen might not be amused at having to go buy another one."

The elevator door opened, and Erika turned to step out just as the red-haired neighbor started to walk in. Erika froze as she saw horror dawn in the woman's eyes.

Only then did she remember that though she'd rubbed off a good deal of the extra makeup in front of the restaurant audience, she hadn't removed it all. Not only did she have a genuine black eye, but she still had two fake bruises on her face and one on her throat.

"My God," the woman said. "I thought...I had no idea...."

"Don't believe everything you see," Amos said grimly. He took Erika's arm and tugged her out of the elevator and toward the door of her apartment.

Erika glanced back as he released the last lock and opened the door. The redhead was still standing in the lobby, her mouth open.

"Oh, that's good," Erika said. "Deny it and manhandle me to the door at the same time."

"What did you want me to do? You were standing there as if you were waiting for her to paint your portrait."

Suddenly, she just felt tired. "Never mind. It was my

fault.'' She sailed the hat onto the top of the pile of wedding gifts on the dining room table. ''I'm going to bed. Tomorrow I'll work out what to do about Felix.''

The car Felix sent to pick them up on Friday evening was a limousine. Erika pulled the deep hood of her cape closely around her face as she walked through the lobby and sank into the plush back seat, grateful for the dark windows which guarded her from casual glances. Amos supervised as the chauffeur loaded their overnight bags, and then slid in beside her. ''I could get used to this,'' he said, leaning forward to inspect the car's accessories as the limo pulled away from the curb.

''Be careful playing with the buttons,'' Erika warned. ''Sometimes they don't do what you'd expect. Where's my briefcase?''

''In the trunk, with your other luggage.''

''I was going to go over my notes again.''

''Don't you already know the plan by heart? You should—you've spent all day on the phone with the lawyers.''

''They kept changing their minds about what I shouldn't say.''

''My very favorite kind of people, lawyers.''

Erika smiled at the irony in his voice. ''Yeah, mine, too. They thrive on creating doubt, confusion, and trouble. And that's exactly why I need to review my notes.''

''Too much cramming for a test can have negative consequences. Sometimes it's more productive to take a break for a pizza.''

''Did that philosophy actually get you through college?''

''Not only college.''

She held her breath, thinking that he might actually confide something of his past.

But he flashed a smile and said, "How do you think I survived a week in training as Stephen's assistant? I wonder if the chauffeur would mind stopping to pick up a pizza to eat on the way."

"I'm sure Felix is planning to give us dinner."

"The question is what Felix considers fit to eat."

She tipped her head to one side and regarded him with honest curiosity. "Why don't you like Felix?"

"Because he's starched stiffer than a dress shirt," Amos said promptly. "I'm betting he shows us to separate bedrooms."

That would solve a number of problems, Erika thought wistfully. "Not a chance. Didn't you hear what he said about not wanting to separate the newlyweds? But as long as we're on the subject, Amos—"

"Of sleeping together? Sweetheart, I knew you'd come around to my way of thinking. And so soon, too."

"Don't get any big ideas. Sharing a room doesn't mean sharing a bed."

He sighed. "I was afraid you were going to be a stickler about it. Where is Felix's country house, anyway?"

"I don't know," Erika said.

"In that case, we should have stopped to get *two* pizzas," Amos said. "One to keep me from starving, and one to toss out the window bit by bit to mark the trail so we can follow it home."

Erika wouldn't have called it a country house, exactly, for though it took a long time in Friday afternoon traffic to get there, Felix's retreat wasn't far from the edge of the city. And it was hardly the cottage she'd expected from his description. *Just a small place, not very exciting—no staff to speak of,* he'd said. But the limo stopped in front of a big, modern glass and steel box set on the edge of a small lake.

"Not your average cabin in the woods," Amos said, eyeing the house. "But at least now I understand why Mr. Urbanity has a country house. In a few years the suburbs will grow up around it, and it'll really be worth a fortune."

Felix opened the door himself and came to greet them. "I hope it was a pleasant drive. Come in and have a drink while George takes care of your luggage."

"My briefcase," Erika said almost automatically. "I'll need—"

"Not tonight," Felix murmured. He led them around a corner and into a big open-plan room with a full wall of glass overlooking the lake. One end of the room held a dining room table already set for three; the other was arranged as a living room with leather couches and chairs. "We'll have a pleasant evening and save business for tomorrow. I'm sure you can entertain yourself while Erika and I are occupied, Amos—may I call you Amos?"

"It won't be difficult for him to keep himself busy," Erika said. "All Amos needs is a place to set up his computer and he'll be quite at home."

Felix smiled as he poured cocktails from an already-prepared pitcher. "What a resourceful and flexible young man you've found for yourself, Erika."

"Darling, didn't I tell you?" Amos said. "I didn't bring my computer."

She frowned. "Why on earth not? You know I'll be busy. You could be working on your book."

"Oh, I brought a notepad so I can jot down ideas. But I didn't want to be distracted by a mere story if you could give me a few minutes now and then."

Felix smiled as if at a private joke. "How very *devout* of you."

Amos was looking around the room, a slightly puzzled expression on his face. Erika wondered what had seized his attention. There wasn't much to look at, really; the room was minimally furnished in glass, leather, and steel. The only spots of color were a couple of modern paintings on the wall opposite the lake view.

"What's the matter?" she asked quietly.

"I was just thinking that the modern touches must reflect Felix's taste, since Kate's ran more to lacy and frilly stuff."

Erika felt as if she'd been kicked. "How would you know what Kate's taste was like?"

Amos shrugged. "I'm just judging by the picture of her on the shampoo bottles."

"There's a big difference between taste and image," Felix said. "Taste is personal. Image is all a part of marketing."

"I beg your pardon," Amos said. "I'm sure it's a painful subject still, and I shouldn't have brought it up."

Felix nodded stiffly. "I'm going to check with the cook about how dinner's progressing. But first I'll show you to your rooms to freshen up."

Erika was so relieved he hadn't simply thrown them out that for a moment she didn't even register that he'd said *rooms.*

She was touching up her makeup when the door of her suite opened and Amos came in.

"I don't believe I heard you knock," she said, concentrating on blending in an extra layer of foundation.

"That's because I didn't," he said cheerfully. "Like Felix said, it's all just part of the image—popping in to see how my bride is doing. How's the eye?"

"The swelling's finally gone, so at least I have a fighting chance of covering it up. But the bruised area just seems to absorb makeup."

"Felix didn't say a word about it. Odd."

"You think everything about Felix is odd."

"And I'm right. You owe me, by the way, since I won the bet about the separate bedrooms."

"I didn't bet."

"Yes, you did. But if you insist, I'll offer you a deal. Double or nothing says Kate didn't know he had this little retreat in the woods."

"What? Because of the furniture? That's ridiculous. Anyway, you're the one who said Felix is too proper. He wouldn't—"

"No, I said he's starched. He only appears to be proper—it's all marketing. See you at dinner."

But no matter what Amos believed, Erika thought Felix was the perfect host at dinner that evening. The following morning, after a leisurely breakfast, he made sure that Amos had a list of the nearby shops, directions to the walking path which circled the lake and a guest card to the nearest gym.

But Amos was obviously in no hurry to get any exercise. For a guy who'd been complaining about not being able to leave the apartment, he seemed oddly content to bench-press the morning newspaper just outside the nook off the living room which Felix had set up as a home office.

By mid-morning, the occasional rustle of the paper seemed to be wearing on Felix's nerves. "I'd have thought the man could take a hint," he fumed. "This puppy-dog devotion of his is really beyond the limits, you know."

Erika bit her lip. "Why don't you go get yourself a fresh cup of coffee? I'll talk to him."

She waited till Felix was out of earshot, then walked into the living room and leaned against the back of a chair, her arms folded across her chest.

Amos didn't look up from the newspaper. Erika would have sworn it was the same page he'd been reading an hour earlier when she'd walked through to get her notebook.

"Making much progress?" he asked.

"As a matter of fact, no. Felix seems a little distracted this morning."

"Really? I'd have said he was disorganized, myself. It sounds as if most of what he wants has already been covered in the fine print."

Erika glared at him. "You've been listening?"

"Well, it is a little difficult not to overhear when—"

"That does it! Go outside and play—I'll call you in time for lunch. Maybe."

She thought he might argue, but he didn't. He took his time, though, folding the newspaper to precisely its original shape before he left the room.

Erika went back into the little study. A couple of minutes later Felix returned with two cups of coffee. "Wonderful," he said. "I'm glad you made things clear to him. I must say I didn't think he'd take my comment seriously about not separating the newlyweds. He simply can't have understood that he was way outside his role, here."

She was looking at the notebook page where she'd been listing Felix's questions. "Of course he had no business listening, but—"

"Oh, I don't think he's any kind of industrial spy. It's just that we hardly need a chaperone."

"No, we don't," she said absently. "I believe we were discussing packaging, Felix. I thought I'd been clear right from the beginning of the negotiations that I intended to keep all of Kate's designs for bottles and boxes—"

"Yes, yes, of course you were clear. You know, it was very clever of you to actually get married, Erika. As long as you're parading a handsome husband around in public, nobody will wonder what else you might be doing and with whom. And now that he's finally gotten the message that there are limits to his job—" Felix gave the papers a push.

"Well, there's no need to go through the motions anymore, is there?"

Erika couldn't believe what she was hearing. "Motions?"

"Now we can get down to the real business of the weekend. Shall we continue our...negotiations...in your suite, or mine?"

"I have no intention of sleeping with you, if that's what you have in mind."

"Why did you ask for a private meeting if you didn't intend it to be private?"

Erika put two fingertips to the side of her face, but she didn't even try to explain her black eye. Felix wouldn't believe her anyway. "You were upset about the gossip linking the two of us," she said. "You said you weren't interested in me."

"No," he corrected. "I said I wouldn't be pushed into marrying you. After one miserable marriage, I'm not about to take on another spoiled princess—not legally, at least. But now that you've neatly taken care of that obstacle as well as the gossip, I can't think of a single reason why we can't have fun."

Erika was speechless.

"Can't you?" said a low, even voice from right behind her. "I can." Amos stepped into the archway between the living room and the study. "Gather up your stuff, Erika. There's a car out front, and your suitcase is already in it."

She gaped at him for an instant and then mechanically began to pile papers into her briefcase. Her fingers were trembling too much to snap the locks, and Amos reached over her shoulder and did it. With his arm still around her, he faced Felix. "You'll deal with the attorneys from now on, La Croix. Keep your hands off my wife. And don't breathe a word about any of this, or I will personally make sure you regret it.''

Erika stumbled on the way to the car, and Amos picked her up, briefcase and all, and carried her the rest of the way.

Her cape was spread across the seat of a small white convertible. The top was down, and the sunlight had warmed the forest-green wool. He folded it around her like a blanket. ''Are you all right?''

She nodded. ''I just can't believe I didn't see what he was. He seemed so devoted to Kate.''

''Marketing,'' Amos said crisply.

''I guess so. Where did you get this car?''

''Called the rental place first thing this morning and had it delivered. I packed while you were getting settled down to work after breakfast.''

''You knew he was going to hit on me.''

''Yep.''

''How?''

He didn't look at her. ''I just knew.''

I'm betting he shows us to separate bedrooms, Amos had said. *Double or nothing says Kate didn't know he had this little retreat in the woods.*

The tires screeched a bit as he pulled out of the driveway, and Amos eased off the gas. ''Nice little car,'' he said. ''A convertible, a pretty girl, sunshine...all we need is a picnic and we'd have a perfect day.''

''I think I just want to go home.''

He didn't answer, but he turned toward the city.

The tires clicked steadily over seams in the concrete, and the rhythm began to build in Erika's head. It all seemed so inevitable now, looking back....

''I caused a lot of trouble for nothing,'' she said finally.

''No, you caused a lot of trouble to get Kate's company.

And you'll still get it. Felix may be slimy, but he's practical.''

She wasn't so sure she agreed. But she was a little surprised to find that she didn't care much any more whether she acquired Kate La Croix's business or not. Had she ever cared?

Yes, she told herself, she had. What she didn't know for sure was when all that had changed. When had her main ambition ceased to be getting Kate's formulas? When had the goal become to keep Amos, instead?

The night at the literacy banquet, when he'd slipped a diamond on her finger? Or before that, over a hot dog in the park?

Not that it mattered. It had happened, and that was all that counted. She had been susceptible from the beginning. She had been unaccustomed to being close to a man who was helpful, a man who wanted to protect her. There was Stephen of course, and she'd come to count on him—but Stephen could never have been a danger to her heart. Amos, on the other hand—well, Amos had never been anything but dangerous.

From their first encounter, *Amos darling* had been different. He'd been a threat in ways she'd only dimly understood, and he'd been a challenge as well. That was why she hadn't had enough sense to avoid him. Why she'd kept going back. Why, even after he'd turned her down and explained how totally loopy her idea was, she'd asked him again...

The apartment seemed chilly, even though they'd been gone only overnight. She stood in the foyer shivering while Amos picked up the mail which had been dropped through the slot in the door. ''Oh, look. Here's the bill for your ring.'' He tore the envelope open and glanced inside, and his eyebrows lifted. ''Stephen has even better taste than I gave him credit for." He tossed the pile of mail on the hall table.

"Thank you for rescuing…" Erika's throat tightened, and she couldn't finish the sentence.

"Just doing my job, ma'am." His tone was light.

She couldn't let it go on any longer. It already hurt so much that she couldn't look at him. "I don't care any more what Felix thinks or what the tabloids say. You don't have to stay, Amos. I'll keep my end of our bargain."

The silence in the little foyer was suddenly more intense than any noise she'd ever heard.

"I don't have to leave, either." His voice was gruff.

"Don't tease me. I can't stand it."

"I'm not teasing, sweetheart. It's up to you."

For a long moment both of them were still. Then he held out an arm, inviting her close. She didn't consciously choose to go to him, but before Erika knew it she was in his arms.

His previous kisses had shaken her, but this one was off the scale. He kissed her slowly, like a man who was approaching a loaded buffet table fully intending to take his time and sample everything on offer. But what he roused in her was beyond mere appetite. She was starving—and only he could satisfy her hunger pangs. Her knees went weak, and he caught her as she slid.

"I'm getting in the habit of carrying you around," he murmured against her lips.

And then they were in her bedroom, and together—and there was nothing more to say.

It was Tuesday before Erika came out of the apartment, and then only because the lawyers insisted on a face-to-face conference to discuss her meeting with Felix.

"What are you going to tell them?" Amos asked. He

was sitting by the kitchen table with a coffee cup cradled in his hand, wearing nothing but jeans, his hair still ruffled from when he'd rolled over to kill the alarm clock and Erika had pulled him down to her.

"Besides that he's a scumbag? I haven't thought that far."

"Had too many other things on your mind lately?" he asked lazily.

I haven't got a mind anymore, she thought. *Only random thoughts of you.* "It's just as well, you know. I have to go back to work sometime, and so do you."

"Come on, honey. You promised to make sure I'd finish the book in less than the forty-five years I thought it would take. So it's forty years instead—what difference does half a decade make here or there?" And then he kissed her goodbye so thoroughly that she almost forgot where she was going.

And that, of course, was the question. Where were they headed?

Certainly not toward anything permanent. Despite his tantalizing farewell, Erika knew better than even to think about forever. A fire as hot as the one that burned between them couldn't last for always—in fact, she suspected it might already have been quenched if it hadn't been for the tight guard she had kept on herself all weekend. She had not sought promises, she had not asked questions, she had not allowed any conversation which hinted of a future beyond the next meal.

But she knew that sooner or later, the La Croix deal would be finished, one way or the other, and Amos would grow restive, and it would all be over.

She had made a promise, and she would keep it. And part of that promise was not to tell him that it wasn't just a matter of fun for her, that her heart would break when he went.

When she stepped into her office, Kelly was just setting a cappuccino on the desk, next to a pile of mail stacked atop a folded newspaper. For a moment, Erika felt as if time had folded in on itself and the last couple of weeks had been nothing but a dream. "You're a wonder, Kelly." She took a sip and flipped through the open letters. "What does the *Sentinel* have to say this time?"

"About you? Nothing. They're maintaining a dignified silence, pretending not to notice that all the other papers are laughing at them."

"Well, that makes a nice change."

"But it seems Denby Miles and his fiancée had the obligatory prenuptial fight at the theater over the weekend, and someone happened to catch it on film. So the *Sentinel* won't be going out of the gossip business for a few more days at least. Phillippa Strang called, by the way. She wants a couple of minutes this morning."

"I do not want to talk to an agent today, Kelly. If she hasn't figured out by now that I'm not going to write the story of my life—"

A throaty smoker's voice interrupted from the doorway. "You're not? That's certainly an interesting twist. I suppose you think that just collaborating, rather than putting your name on the cover, makes a difference." The chubby woman with the impossibly black hair looked older and more worn than she had at the literacy banquet. "Sorry to walk in on you like this, but if you don't want people to overhear you, you should shut the door completely."

Erika counted to ten. "Good morning, Phillippa. Since you heard me already, there's no point in going over it all again. And I am a bit busy today, so—"

"I asked you for that book. It was my idea, my project,

my baby. You should have the good manners to offer it to me first."

"I don't know what you're talking about, but I have no intention of writing the story of my life, or collaborating, or anything else."

Phillippa's jaw jutted out stubbornly. "Then how do you explain Amos Abernathy?"

The question was so ridiculous that Erika almost burst out laughing. "Explain him? Why should I have to explain him?"

Phillippa studied her for a long time, her eyes narrowed. "If you really don't know, then maybe you need to ask him to explain himself. Have him tell you why he meets with his editor in the back corner of a bar instead of in the publisher's office."

"Amos has an editor?" Erika asked feebly.

"And why they were talking about you."

"Really, Phillippa, it's no secret we got married."

"He wasn't describing the wedding. You might also inquire why he's been asking so many questions about you, and your father, and the company. Grilling everybody around you." She shot a glance at Kelly. "Including you—am I right?"

Kelly gulped. "I wouldn't call it grilling. Of course he's interested—"

"He was quizzing you about me?" Erika asked. "Not talking about you?"

"That's what makes him good, you know," Phillippa went on. "People want to talk to him."

Kelly was biting her lip, Erika saw. Looking guilty.

"It seems to me, Erika my girl, that either you know what he's doing, or you don't. And if you don't—well, then, that boy has himself one heck of a scoop. *Up Close and Personal*—I understand from my source in the publisher's office that's the working title. Sound like it might apply to anyone you know?''

CHAPTER TEN

PHILLIPPA was wrong, that was all, Erika told herself. Dead wrong.

So what if Amos was going around asking questions about her? He had a right to be inquisitive. Besides, he couldn't have been asking all that many questions—he hadn't had time. Locked up in the apartment for days on end...

With a telephone and a computer, she reminded herself. What had he been doing, all those hours he'd been shut in the den? Writing? Or asking questions?

If he was curious about the woman he'd married, that was understandable. Come to that, there were a few things—make that a lot of things—that she'd like to know about him. But why would he have been investigating her father, and Ladylove?

Up Close and Personal...

Had he been so eager for her to outwit the *Sentinel* because he wanted to protect her, or because he wanted to keep the tabloid from breaking any more stories about her so he could explode the bombshells himself?

You don't know that any of this is true. Stop jumping to conclusions. Phillippa's wrong—she's got to be.

This time the agent's source had made a mistake. That had to be what had happened. Erika shook her head. "Amos is writing a novel, not an exposé."

But was she certain of that? She had assumed it was fiction, and she couldn't remember whether Stephen had ever said it was a novel. However, she was pretty sure that

Amos had always referred to it as "a book"—and that was a definition which covered a great deal more territory.

But that wasn't all Stephen had said, she remembered. *Amos is writing a book. That's why he's here.*

What if it wasn't the flexible hours and free living quarters which had been the job's attraction, but the proximity to the subject of his investigation?

"Maybe he was writing a novel," Phillippa said, "until he saw a chance to do something a whole lot more lucrative."

Erika had to make an effort to keep her voice steady. "How do you know all this, Phillippa?"

"I happened to be in the bar last Wednesday morning when he and his editor were having coffee."

The day of the photo shoot, Erika thought. The day of her accident. But Amos hadn't showed up in the studio till later—he could have had a dozen appointments before that.

"I recognized Amos from the banquet," Phillippa went on, "and the editor from doing business with him a few years ago. And I overheard bits of the conversation. They were talking about advances, and contracts, and you."

Advances and contracts... Had Amos sold his book? But if so, why hadn't he shared the good news? Erika could think of only one reason why he wouldn't have told her, and it sent her heart sinking like a freight elevator—slow but inexorable.

"So then I dropped a question to a friend at the publishing house about what that particular editor is working on these days, and he told me there's a very hush-hush project called *Up Close and Personal.* He said the author's been undercover to do the research."

Undercover. Well, that would be an interesting way to describe Amos's life lately....

What did she really know about Amos, anyway? Not

very much, when it came right down to it. But she'd thought his being nobody special would help protect her. She had never realized it might be a disguise that he'd assumed on purpose. It hadn't occurred to her that it might be a threat to her.

There was something very like pity in Phillippa's eyes. "Sorry, kid. I hate to be the one to ruin your day."

Erika was glad the woman walked out of the office without waiting to be thanked. It would have choked her to say the words.

As the door closed behind the agent, Kelly took a deep breath. "Oh, Erika—what are you going to do?"

Erika pushed herself up from her chair. "Meet with the lawyers," she said. "I still have a job to do."

The meeting didn't take long, since her discussion with Felix had brought up no issues of substance and led to no changes in the proposed buyout. Erika's team of attorneys spent most of the time trying to puzzle out why Felix had made a big deal out of nothing.

Erika didn't enlighten them. She wasn't eager just now to tell the world what a fool she'd been. Not seeing through Felix wasn't the biggest part of the problem, of course, but it was a piece of a pattern that she wasn't proud to acknowledge.

You're not cut out to compete with the sharks, Erika, her father's voice whispered in her head. Maybe Stanford Forrester had been right after all—she was too trusting, too apt to take people at face value only to find that they weren't what they had seemed.

But what, exactly, had Amos seemed to be? And how much of that image had been borne in her own imagination?

Most of it, she admitted. He hadn't misled her, exactly.

In fact, he'd said almost nothing about himself. She'd created it all, the whole image. She'd convinced herself that he was what she wanted him to be.

Erika walked home slowly, with the hood of her cloak pulled up despite the warmth of the spring sunshine.

Stephen was in the lobby. She thought about asking him what he knew about Amos, but he was busy with a tenant—and in any case she wasn't sure she wanted to admit, even to Stephen, that she knew so little about the man she had married.

So she merely said hello, and took the package he handed her, and went on upstairs, bracing herself for Amos's greeting.

If he was in the same mood as he'd been for the last few days… Of course, even if that was the case, she told herself philosophically, it wouldn't take long for him to realize that her feelings no longer matched.

Had anything which had happened between them in the last three days been real? Or had even his lovemaking been calculated to keep her off guard, as well as to let him learn her most intimate secrets?

You're assuming he's guilty, she reminded herself. *Wait and see what he has to say for himself.*

The apartment was empty. She knew it the instant she stepped inside.

Her hands were trembling as she hung her cape in the closet, but she didn't hurry. She had the rest of her life to find out for certain that he was gone, so there was no sense in rushing around to confirm what she already knew in her heart.

She'd prepared herself so well that it came as a shock to see that his computer was still on the desk in the den. Wherever he was, then, he was planning to return.

Of course, that didn't mean he was innocent of what

Phillippa had charged. Just that he didn't yet realize that Erika knew he was guilty.

If he's guilty at all, she reminded herself. Her head was starting to hurt with all the unknowns.

Her fingertips itched with the desire to turn the computer on and search for the files that must exist. But she had given her word that she wouldn't sneak a peek at his first draft, and she would keep it.

How very interesting it was, she thought, that he'd extracted that particular promise from her.

But she hadn't promised not to look in the desk. It was still her desk, after all. Her checkbook was in there—the one he'd promised not to look at—and her unpaid bills. She had every right to rummage through the drawers.

She found her check—the one she'd written to him on their wedding night for cash to cover his incidental expenses—in the middle drawer. She wondered if he simply hadn't had time to go to the bank, or if he'd been squeamish about taking her money while he was investigating her. "Though I don't know why he'd flinch at that," she muttered. Her voice seemed to echo in the room.

In a side drawer was a yellow legal pad, covered with scrawled black ink. She recognized it as the one which had been lying on the desk in the office downstairs once, while they'd been talking. He'd said that he felt safe leaving his notes lying around because no one else could read his handwriting—and now she understood his confidence.

Still, no matter how slipshod the handwriting, one's own name was pretty hard to miss, and hers seemed to turn up with regularity among the scrawled and crossed-out sentences. Though she couldn't make out every word, she could read enough to see that what he had written was part observation, part speculation, part analysis, and it went all the way back to the episode of the white silk blouse on the day they had met.

She was still paging through the notebook, reading bits here and there, when she heard his footsteps in the hall.

Amos stopped in the doorway, obviously startled to see her. "You're home earlier than I expected."

"I imagine so."

He took off his jacket and slung it over one shoulder. "If you're upset because I was down the hall—"

"With the redhead? Oh, I'm sure you were only trying to convince her not to talk to the *Sentinel* about the little scene in the elevator a few days ago." She held up the yellow legal pad. "What's this, Amos?"

"My notebook." There was a slight, but very real, emphasis on the possessive. "Why are you reading it?"

"Why shouldn't I? It seems to be all about me. And please don't insult me by expecting me to believe that you were drafting love letters to me, or composing poetry about my beauty. I can't read every word, but I get the gist." She tossed the tablet onto the desk. "I don't suppose you'd like to tell me about *Up Close and Personal?*"

His jaw set. "How do you know about that?"

Erika felt sick. *Then it's true. All of it. Phillippa was right after all.* "Never mind. You have an hour to pack your things. If you're not out by then, I'll have Stephen get security to remove you."

She almost went to her room, but she decided she was damned if she'd hide. She wasn't the one who had something to be ashamed of. So she went to the kitchen instead and made herself a cup of tea that she didn't want. She was standing by the sink dunking the bag and watching the brew turn ever-blacker when Amos came in.

"Erika, would you at least tell me what you're angry about?"

"Don't pretend that you don't know. Contract—editor—advances—*Up Close and Personal.* Is this forming a pattern for you?"

"Yes, but I don't see why you're so angry."

She spun to face him. The tea bag was still in her hand, and hot liquid splattered over the counter. "You don't see why I'm angry? You think I like having my life spread out for public consumption? It's bad enough to have it in the *Sentinel,* but at least that gets thrown out every day. You're going to put it in a book—so it'll stay around forever!"

"Erika, *Up Close and Personal* isn't about you."

"Right. And you have all those notes about me just for fun. Don't insult me, Amos. Just please go away."

"You're going to have to listen to me sometime, you know. There's a little matter of a divorce—and I'm not signing anything until you've heard me out."

"Fine. Don't sign anything. It'll sell an extra million copies of your book if you're still married to me. Anyway, what do I care whether I get a divorce? I'll never make this mistake again." She made a point of looking at the clock. "You're down to forty-five minutes, you know."

He turned on his heel and left the room.

She dumped the tea down the drain, put the bag in the garbage, mopped up the splatters, and stood looking out the window.

Amos came back with a sheaf of paper. "Here's something for you to read while I'm packing."

Erika intended to ignore it. She looked through the mail instead, throwing away the junk and sorting out bills and notes and invitations that had collected over the weekend while she'd been too fascinated with Amos to pay attention to anything else.

But as the minutes ticked away, she found herself looking at the stack of paper—perhaps a hundred typed pages—

lying in an untidy pile on the kitchen table next to the mail. There was, after all, nothing else to do while she waited. And she might as well see what he had to say about her. It would lessen the shock when the book came out.

She didn't read it all, at least not after the first few paragraphs—but she leafed through the stack, looking at every page and reading bits here and there.

By the time Amos came back, she had turned over the last page and was sitting staring at the wall. She didn't move to look at him. "This isn't about me."

"That's what I told you, Erika." He pulled a chair around from the table and straddled it, folding his arms on the back.

"So what is it? Why did you give it to me?"

" It's about the goings-on in an upscale apartment house. There are at least two murders—maybe three before it's over—and a lot of people dodging around trying not to get caught in bedrooms where they don't belong. There's a fashion model and a few society matrons and a manager who's doing his damnedest to figure out who the murderer is before anybody else gets killed—and it will be titled *Up Close and Personal*. If I ever get finished writing it."

"You wrote this?"

"It's not very flattering of you to sound so surprised," he said dryly.

"You're writing a murder mystery."

"Yes."

"Well, you did tell me you weren't setting out to create the Great American Novel." She shook her head. "Why the big secret? It may not be literature but it's nothing to be ashamed of, so why not just tell everybody?"

"You really think I could just introduce myself to the tenants that way? 'Hi, I'm the new manager and I'm going to be watching you very closely because you might end up being a dead body in the book I'm writing.' I don't think that would have been well-received.''

''That's why you took the job? Because you were studying the tenants?''

''You said yourself,'' he reminded, ''that I obviously didn't know much about the kind of people who live in places like this.''

''People like me,'' Erika mused.

''Certainly not enough to write convincingly about them without some observation and research.''

''Was Stephen in on the scheme? How much does he know?''

''Only what he told you—that I took the job for the living arrangements and free time, because I was writing a book.''

''Well, that feels better. At least nobody knew any more than I did.'' She straightened the pile of paper and set it aside with an air of finality. ''So that's why you jumped at the chance to marry me, Amos.''

''If you remember, I didn't exactly jump at the chance,'' he said mildly.

Erika wasn't listening. ''To see things from the inside, as it were. Of course, you couldn't tell me about it then because...because...please do explain why, Amos, because I don't quite get it.''

''Would you have bothered to listen? Would you even have cared, as long as I did what you wanted me to? You seemed to think it was cute, that I was writing a book. *Isn't it precious that Amos thinks he's an author?*''

The accusation stung, because it was partially true. ''And now you are one. Because you've sold the book, haven't you? You were seen meeting with your editor. In a bar. Which brings up another question. Even if I accept the logic for you being here in secret, why is the project so hush-hush for the publisher?''

"Well, that's a little more difficult to explain."

"I've got all night."

"I suppose it's progress," Amos mused, "if you're no longer threatening to throw me out within the next—" he checked his wristwatch "—fifteen minutes."

"Thanks for reminding me of the deadline. And stop trying to avoid the question."

"All right. When my first book came out—"

"Your first book? This isn't your first?"

"Every interruption adds at least a minute to the story," he warned. "When the book was published I used a pen name, because my employer would not have been amused to discover what I'd been doing in my spare time."

Why not? Erika wanted to ask. She bit her tongue instead.

"Now I'm on a leave of absence and hoping to be able to resign when this book is published. But there's always the chance that it'll sell two copies instead of two million, so I might have to go back to my day job."

She couldn't stop herself. "What did you do?"

"I was a corporate lawyer in Denver. A very junior one. Those birds don't think anyone below partner should be allowed any spare time."

My very favorite kind of people, lawyers...

"So the book came out under a different name—" he went on "—and there were no tours, no autographed copies, no public appearances to help the sales. But accidentally, and completely against any logic of publishing, the mystery behind the mystery has increased interest in the first book and also in what Judd Thorne might do next."

"Judd Thorne," she said blankly, and then it clicked.

"The mystery you got as a table favor at the literacy banquet. *With Malice Toward One*—you wrote that?"

"That's why I was trying so hard to give it away that night, or make you leave it behind. I guess I was afraid that if you actually read it, knowing me, you'd see the person behind the pen name."

"But I didn't. It never occurred to me."

"Every time you referred to it as my book, I got a spasm. But I guess you didn't know me as well as I thought you might." A shadow that might have been pain crossed his face.

"Why didn't you tell me?" she whispered, and then answered the question herself, because it was marginally less agonizing to say it than it would be to listen to him explain. "Because there was no need for me to know. I was no different from everybody else."

"That was the reasoning, yes. But once the first opportunity was past, it was too late to say, 'Oh, by the way, Erika, I seem to have forgotten to tell you...'"

She forced a cheerful note into her voice. "So all the notes you were keeping about me—was that just because I'm going to be one of the dead bodies in your book? Virtual murder, as it were? There must have been days when the idea of killing me off was very appealing."

"Not entire days," he corrected. "Moments, maybe."

She bit her lip.

"I'm sorry." The note of humor had vanished from his voice. "Erika, I kept those notes because I was fascinated. I wanted to figure out what made you tick. How a woman could be so utterly gorgeous, and yet value her looks so little. How she could be so capable and strong, and yet think that she was weak."

"A psychological study. Let me know when you get me

figured out—it'll save me the therapy bills. So why did you marry me, Amos?''

For a moment she thought he wasn't going to answer. Then, very soberly, he said, ''Do you want the reason, or the excuse?''

''There's a difference? Successful author of one book, about to be two... You must have laughed at the idea of me paying you a stipend so you could afford to write. But never mind—now I remember. You could get a very different view of the dynamics of the apartment house from this floor than you could from the lobby.''

''That's the excuse,'' he agreed.

''At any rate, it hardly matters now. The lawyers agreed with you—no surprise there, I guess, since it turns out you're one of the same breed. They're sure Felix will agree to the deal. I guess it doesn't matter any more, whatever the *Sentinel* says.''

''So this is the end?''

''Well, the bargain we made was only till the sale went through, and that seems close enough now. I'm sure you'll appreciate having peace and quiet to write. You must have gotten almost nothing done this week—except a lot of research.''

''I certainly learned a lot,'' he said soberly.

''Me, too. Thanks for sticking around to explain. It's been...quite instructive. And thanks for the week.'' She'd intended to keep it light, flippant, but her voice cracked. ''I'd say it's been fun, but...''

''What do you want, Erika?''

You, her heart cried. But what was the point in saying it? Would she get some sort of masochistic satisfaction from hearing him explain why he wasn't interested? ''My life back,'' she said.

He sat very still for a moment longer, and then stood up

and pushed the chair neatly into place with a movement that was so economical it was just short of violent. "Then I'll finish my packing."

"Don't forget this," she said, and pushed the stack of paper toward him. "And there's a bill somewhere in that pile for you, too. Your credit card, I believe."

He looked straight at her, his eyes blazing. "And to think that I actually believed Denby Miles was an idiot to let go of you."

"What?"

"But the *Sentinel* was right about that one. You led him on to get those formulas, and then you dumped him. Maybe Felix wasn't so wrong after all, to be wary of your intentions."

"Get out," she said.

"It's a good thing your father's dead," he said, and suddenly he didn't sound angry any more, only tired. He started to shuffle through the papers on the table. "Because I want to kill him for what he did to you. For making you believe you weren't good enough, no matter what you did. For making you into a robot."

She swallowed hard and closed her eyes against the tears.

"What's this?" he said.

She looked, and tried to stifle a gasp. He was holding a small box, the package Stephen had given her when she came in this afternoon. She had dropped the box on the table on her way to the den, and then pushed it aside so she could sort the mail. And in the press of emotions, she'd forgotten it was there. "Nothing," she said. "Give it here, please."

"It's got my name on it," he pointed out.

She watched, frozen, as he lifted the lid off the box. She saw the exact instant when he recognized the contents, because he looked from the box to her left hand. "It's a match for yours," he said. "A wedding ring. But why, Erika?"

She shook her head. Even if she'd known what she wanted to say, she couldn't have formed the words and forced them out.

He set the box on the edge of the table as carefully if it were a soap bubble and came toward her. "You asked a question a few minutes ago—why I married you. You know the excuse. Do you want to hear the reason?"

No, she thought. *I don't want to be tormented anymore.*

Amos had never laid a hand on her in anger or violence, only in passion and—perhaps—affection. He'd never belittled her as her father had, or made light of her talents. She didn't believe he'd ever intended to hurt her. It had all been research for him—not a joke, exactly, but hardly earth-shaking.

It was Erika who had let it be important. When she fell in love with him, she'd given him the power to hurt her worse than any other person in the world ever had, or ever could. It wasn't fair to blame Amos for that, when it had been her own doing.

But she didn't have to listen to anything more. She didn't have to add to her pain.

"You were fascinated." She pushed back her chair and stood up. "You told me that already."

"That's part of it," he said. "But the reason I was fascinated was something I didn't begin to understand until it was too late. I expected you to be like your photos—perfect and cold. Stephen tried to tell me you weren't that way at all. But he didn't warn me about how easy it would be to fall in love with you."

"I don't believe you." Her voice was little more than a croak.

"I don't expect you to. But it's true. I didn't know what

was happening to me. I only knew that I wanted to keep you safe and to take care of you. And even when I realized what I was feeling—well, how could I tell you that I'd fallen head over heels in love with you? You told me once you'd have to be a fool to believe that—and the one thing you aren't, Erika, is a fool. When did you buy the ring, sweetheart? And why?''

There was a softness in his voice, a sadness, that wrapped around her heart and squeezed until she could do nothing but tell the truth. ''I asked Stephen to get it, just this morning. Because I want so badly for it all to be real.''

Suddenly he closed the gap between them, and she was in his arms, and he was kissing her with a passionate fury which threatened to turn her to cinders. ''I love you,'' she managed to whisper, once—and then she couldn't say anything more at all.

It was much later that she remembered the ring and slid it onto his finger. ''With this ring, I—'' she said. ''Oh, I don't remember the rest. But you know what I mean.''

He gave a howl of laughter and kissed her again, with a easy possessiveness which sent thrills up her spine. ''Don't let me forget to pay that bill,'' she said. ''For my ring, I mean. You said it came, but I didn't see it in the stack.''

''That's because I paid it this morning. A man can't have his wife buying her own diamond ring. Of course, I'm going to have to tell Stephen his good taste is why I can't afford to give him a Christmas bonus, but—''

''I'm sure he won't hold it against you. Just to set things straight, by the way, Denby Miles never wanted to be married to me. He wanted to be the president of Ladylove, and he was willing to trade his formulas and marry the heiress if that was the price to get the job. He'd hoped to have it all accomplished, to worm his way in—but my father died very suddenly, and Denby gave himself away.''

"So you ditched him and kept the job. Good girl."

"That's about the size of it. He was furious when I told the board that I wouldn't agree to him having the job because I wanted it myself. The really funny thing was—I didn't want it. At least, I didn't think I did at first."

"And you didn't think you were capable," Amos added. "Because your father told you that you were nothing more than a pretty face, and that while your mother was beautiful, you were…adequate."

"You have done your research." But somehow, when he said it, the phrase didn't sting. She felt sad, but no longer diminished. "Maybe you're right and it's time for a new Face of Ladylove."

"Later," he said. "We'll talk about that later."

"Or maybe lots of faces. Smiling ones, imperfect ones, all colors, all sizes—" But he was kissing her, and she forgot what she was talking about. It was a long time before she came up for air. "There's just one more thing, *Amos darling*. I couldn't help but notice, as I was reading *Up Close and Personal*…"

"Yes?" He sounded absentminded, because he was nibbling on her earlobe.

"You told me you were working on a love scene—but there is no love scene in the book."

"Did I say it was for the book?" he whispered against her lips. "Sorry, sweetheart. Let me make it up to you."

And he pulled her closer and showed her exactly what he meant.

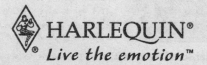

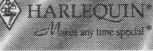

The world's bestselling romance series.

HARLEQUIN®
Presents

Seduction and Passion Guaranteed!

THE PRINCESS BRIDES

For duty, for money…for passion!

Discover a thrilling new trilogy from a rising star of Harlequin
Presents®, Jane Porter!

Meet the Royals…

Chantal, Nicolette and Joelle are members of the blue-blooded
Ducasse family. Step inside their sophisticated and glamorous
world and watch as these beautiful princesses find they have
to marry three international playboys—for duty, for money…
and definitely for passion!

Don't miss

THE SULTAN'S BOUGHT BRIDE (#2418)
September 2004

THE GREEK'S ROYAL MISTRESS (#2424)
October 2004

THE ITALIAN'S VIRGIN PRINCESS (#2430)
November 2004

**Pick up a Harlequin Presents® novel and you will enter a world
of spine-tingling passion and provocative, tantalizing romance!**

Available wherever Harlequin books are sold.

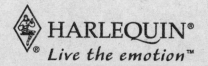

HARLEQUIN®
Live the emotion™

www.eHarlequin.com

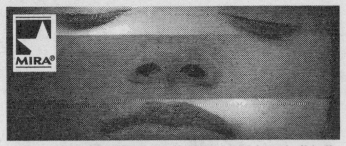

"Twisted villains, dangerous secrets...irresistible."
—*Booklist*

New York Times Bestselling Author

STELLA CAMERON

Just weeks after inheriting Rosebank, a once-magnificent Louisiana plantation, David Patin was killed in a mysterious fire, leaving his daughter, Vivian, almost bankrupt. With few options remaining, Vivian decides to restore the family fortunes by turning Rosebank into a resort hotel.

Vivan's dream becomes a nightmare when she finds the family's lawyer dead on the sprawling grounds of the estate. Suddenly Vivian begins to wonder if her father's death was really an accident...and if the entire Patin family is marked for murder.

Rosebank is not in Sheriff Spike Devol's jurisdiction, but Vivian, fed up with the corrupt local police, asks him for unofficial help. The instant attraction between them leaves Spike reluctant to get involved—until another shocking murder occurs and it seems that Vivian will be the next victim.

kiss them goodbye

"Cameron returns to the wonderfully atmospheric Louisiana setting...for her latest sexy-gritty, compellingly readable tale of romantic suspense."—*Booklist*

Available the first week of October 2004,
wherever paperbacks are sold!

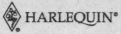